The Dutch Doll

by

Philip Snow

Grosvenor House
Publishing Limited

Philip Snow is hereby identified as author of this
work in accordance with Section 77 of the Copyright, Designs
and Patents Act 1988

The book cover picture is copyright to Daniele Serra

This book is published by
Grosvenor House Publishing Ltd
28-30 High Street, Guildford, Surrey, GU1 3HY.
www.grosvenorhousepublishing.co.uk

A CIP record for this book
is available from the British Library

ISBN 978-1-906210-14-4

Printed by Biddles Ltd, King's Lynn, Norfolk

*To Tina, who helped to sustain
the writing of this ghost story.
It frightened me in the course of its
construction; it should do the same for you.*

An old waist-high Dutch Doll is stolen from a village church. Its theft reopens old wounds and uncovers local folklore. Of how the doll was kept in the cellar of the Girl's School, scene of a tragedy in the 1930's and at the centre of ghostly rumours a century before. They say that the doll's feet were cut off to stop it walking around. Only the narrator of the story and the vicar understand the forces at work; only they are on the doll's trail. Based on a true story. The real Dutch Doll is still at large.

"The goods were all moved from the house,
The children sleep away"

Moving silently, without resistance, across wet red clay.
The merest hint of dawn touched the far hedgerows. The
steeple, retreating into the distance, held no power now.

I

[1981]

Back under the yew tree, lay the four hessian sacks. Inside the church, Neale and Abbott moved without
lights or words. Heels muffled, they communicated by
means of touch and gesture, illuminated only by the
deep magenta glow through the leaded memorials.
They had chosen a night with a full moon with good
reason.

The doll stood, as it had for the last forty seven years,
on her small wooden plinth. She was about three feet
tall, carved in a puritan style, as a schoolgirl of the eigh-
teenth century. She wore a bonnet and her face had
simple, sharp features; a thin nose, round eyes and high
painted brow. Her blue dress, a continuation of the carving, was a laced bodice and then a wider flowing skirt
reaching down to her ankles. And her ankles were all

1

that there was - there were no feet. In one hand, tucked under her right arm, she held a bible. In the other, there was a scroll boldly commanding: "SearcH ye the ScriP-TuRes". She was fixed to the wall by iron reins, fitted loosely over each shoulder, so you could move her an inch or two within her confines.

Abbott worked with his crowbar, moving deftly around the effigy. He snapped one fastening without much sound and masonry dusted his boot. With more leverage the ironwork was wrenched from the stone and clattered to the floor. An unholy tuneless ringing reverberated about the vaulted nave.

"Watch it!" Neale whispered with an oath and added spittle. The two both waited for a moment, glancing hesitantly at the heavy oak door. Neale even ventured over and listened against the wood. With wary eyes, he trod softly back to the far wall and gave Abbott a silent nod. Abbott set to work again. Quickly, the second shackle was twisted and pulled from the wall and placed gingerly against the back of a pew. Neale placed one hand on the belly of the doll to steady her as this was done. Finally, he hoisted her onto his shoulder.

Neale didn't notice and Abbott was busy packing away his tools, but a slight, barely perceptible smile formed on the doll's lips. It stirred the whole building, again in a subtle way that wasn't noticeable to the pre-occupied men. The church bible, on the golden eagle lectern as it always was, skipped a few pages as though turned by a breeze, and yet the door was closed.

A little girl's voice in the pulpit said, "Search ye the scriptures", and began reciting further from John's gospel, "for in them ye think ye have eternal life: and they are they which testify of me."

But Abbott and Neale saw and heard none of this. They had their prize, their minds were fixed on money and they were oblivious.

The church clock was chiming half past midnight. I heard it too; half asleep, troubled by dreams and uncomfortable. The old house was creaking and shifting, as it always seemed to in the small hours. We'd moved in less than five months before, my wife Louise, daughter Emily and I. A dream come true. A large old school-house. Georgian and solidly made of local ironstone, it stood on a bank above the road, barely fifty yards from the church gate. We had settled in well, but my insomnia had worsened and I still hadn't got used to the house's nocturnal moans. I expect that they sounded during the day too, but I noticed them most of all when the rest of the household was breathing deeply. They were then, as I struggled with the covers and listened out.

A sharp crack of timber made me prick up my ears. I was unsure whether it was inside or out. A wind was getting up, so it wasn't impossible that it was the trees outside. Then there is was again. And again. Like someone was coming up the stairs. Well, we all have those kinds of feelings - that an unwelcome someone is in the house at night. And I'm fairly rational, so I dismissed that thought as soon as it entered my head. But I shuddered and pulled up the covers in any case. Just then, I was seized by the most excruciating cramps in both legs. Calf and ankle muscles contracted and knotted in a heartbeat rhythm. I stretched out my feet and forced them against the footboard to get some relief. With a sudden gasp that reached deep down into my chest, I realised that I wasn't in my old bed and that this one was open at the foot. I recoiled under the quilt.

Drawing in a deep breath through my nostrils and hearing another sharp crack and what sounded like scuffling, I sat up abruptly. Burning.

I tore back the covers and shook Louise. "I can smell burning", I whispered. She was awake in an instant. "What!" she cried, jumping up and making for Emily's room. I was quickly climbing into a pair of jeans and switched on the stairway light. There was movement at the bottom, I thought…no; there was a flickering, definitely a fire coming from the kitchen. I ushered Louise and Emily down the stairs and along the hallway towards the front door. Light, noise and heat were all much more intense at the doorway leading down three more steps into the kitchen, scullery and cellar. I slammed the door shut and paused for a second, thinking just for a moment about anything else I needed, anything else I should do. As I stood there, there were three loud hammering sounds in quick succession, followed by the sound of breaking glass. Something must have exploded.

Nick Sinclaire, the vicar, sat at his kitchen table, writing, with a large King James bible to the left of his paper and a miscellany of other books of differing size and condition strewn about him. He was deep in thought, obviously struggling to find words, holding his glasses in one hand and rubbing his eyes with the other. When he heard me knock at the open door, he looked up, immediately gave a friendly smile; the one, I suspected, that he produced automatically for parishioners regardless of his real mood.

"Ah, hello!", still warm and perhaps less automatic, "I'm so very sorry to hear about your catastrophe. What with that and our drama and the dreadful accident on the Harrowden road, I'd be surprised if anyone within half a mile of the church got any sleep last night." My bemusement must have been plain to see. "Haven't you heard? Well, I suppose with your own emergency to contend with, you could hardly be expected to keep a count of the number of sirens whirling around you. We in the vicarage were woken by a terrible banging sound. I thought that someone was up to no good in the church-yard again. You'll know about that sickening piece of defilement a couple of months ago?" I nodded gravely. "Anyway, I got Fred up and we went over, unarmed save for my protector and Fred's gardening shovel. By the time we got to the West door, we could hear a....howling sound is the only way I can describe it, as though some sort of animal was trapped inside the church. So it was with much trepidation and nervous shaking of keys in locks, that we came in through the bell tower. The noise stopped abruptly and we were aware of running feet outside and a car starting up. We just rushed out in time to see this red thing - I'm useless with car models - careering up Church Lane. I phoned the police straight away. We had a good look around and it was then that we realised that they'd taken the Dutch doll. Nothing else; the silverware was in the safe of course. But the candlesticks and collection plates - quite valuable - all present and correct."

"And the accident on the Harrowden road?"

"That was the worst of all. They must have been going at some speed to get away. The two thieves that is. Crashed headlong into a tree and the motor exploded.

5

Neither stood a chance. Then within the hour, your place was going up. You poor people."

By now the vicar was messily gathering his things together and inviting me over to the church. I told him about our need to get a place for Louise and Emily to stay. He offered to put them up at the vicarage, "...the more the merrier and we have plenty of room. And what about you?"

"Oh, I need to stay on at the house. There were only two rooms seriously damaged by fire and because the burglar alarm is out of action it's only wise..."

"I suppose so. But you're most welcome to join us for meals and so forth."

"Thank you."

We skirted around the North side of the church and I imagined, as I often quite morbidly do, myself standing by these graves, fresh dug, before Joshua, Hannah and Mary were buried, before the grey slate bearing their names were erected, and before the lichen and the ivy encroached.

"They got in through here", said Nick, taking me through the splintered priest's door, "and it's been a devil of a job getting in to tidy up. The police were finger-printing and so on and only left about an hour ago." He had the habit, I noticed, of taking the devil's name in vain. His way of mocking Satan, I assumed. He pointed out the holes in the wall at the rear, the metal shackles and scattered mortar. "Whether they only had designs on her, or were disturbed and left before gathering together their planned hoard, I don't know. They must have been after the lectern too, because the bible was on the floor. But other than that and the door, we escaped unscathed..."

"Which is more that they did", I cut in.

6

"Yes, poor souls. And though I love this church and treasure it's contents, I forgive them their trespass, if you'll forgive the pun. They certainly didn't deserve what happened to them. They're being judged now and it's not my place to pre-empt the Almighty."

"You know the story of the Dutch doll, of course", Nick went on. I said I did in outline, but wanted to hear his version. "It lived in your house until 1934, when the old Girl's School closed down. Where it came from, no one really knows. It had been at the school since the 1820's. I think it might have been commissioned or purchased by the original proprietor, because it dates from about that time - it's dress was in the style of the period. There were stories of the schoolhouse being haunted in...1824 and the vicar at the time famously preached on the subject of the evils of witchcraft on three successive Sundays. Three girls were implicated and accused of making the noises themselves. Finally there was an exorcism, the girls were expelled and that was the end of the matter. They say that the Dutch Doll had it's feet cut off to stop it walking around. But the slur on the school lingered. There were stories that the doll was kept in the cellar and girls locked in there with it for punishment. That it was still - animated - and was a harbinger of all manner of wickedness." Nick smiled cynically. "Tales of this sort abound for over a hundred years until the eve of the school's closure. The last Head-mistress, a formidable character by the name of Miss Mary Ozier, suffered terrific nightmares and this lead somehow to the doll being placed in the church."

I wanted to tell him about my own dreams, but I was afraid of looking a fool. The last thing I wanted was to add to some nineteenth century hysteria.

"So it's theft is just the latest chapter in a long and chequered history" I said.

"And more to come, I expect", Nick replied, "You see, it wasn't in the car when they found it. I think they must have dropped it in their haste. Or perhaps they thought they were being pursued and threw it out of the car before they crashed. The police have conducted quite a detailed search along it's route and there's no trace. Someone must have spotted an opportunity and taken it. And there's something else worrying me about the accident."

"What's to worry about - the weather was pretty bad and that lane is not the easiest to navigate in the dark..."

"Yes, but there's something peculiar about where the car came off the road."

So we got into the vicar's old Landrover and took a ride along the Harrowden Road. The sky was overcast and faint drizzle dappled the windscreen. Through a narrow stretch of road, hemmed in by an avenue of elms, then out into the open and down hill towards the river. Beyond that, and on the opposite side of the valley, the railway embankment. As we drove down the hill, I could see crows disturbed and unsettled, circling the winter fingers of the spinney. Ahead, the scorched tree with a web of police tape.

"Looks nasty", I said, "I'm not surprise no one walked away." Although the car had been removed, there was a deep gouge in the earth and a hole in the side of the tree, blackened and angry looking.

"Mmm", replied Nick, deep in thought, "but it was something else that I wanted you to see." He climbed the bank on the other side and beckoned me to join him. "Can you see where we are, where the car halted?" He drew a line with his forearm at right angles to the road, beyond the tree, then back behind us towards the spinney. "It's not just that this tree is in the corner of the field and that there's another field border behind us - these hedges are ancient; been here for hundreds of years. And I checked some maps in the church library this morning. These hedges mark the old parish boundary. You didn't see the wreckage. It looked as though the car had been stopped suddenly by some devilish force. More than just the damage caused by it hitting the tree. This may sound outlandish, I know, but it was as if some malevolent barrier was preventing it from leaving the parish."

And the rain came on heavy.

At the schoolhouse, the insurance assessor having been and gone, I was trying to tidy up. I was taking out lumps of charred wood that used to be my kitchen. As I added to the heap in the front lawn, I was spied by Mrs Hinde. She was the old widow from across at one of the (former) charity cottages. She looked over eighty. A pronounced stoop dominated her form, her face and hands were heavily liver-spotted, but her eyes were still bright green and lively. She always wore black, though she said that her husband had been dead for over twenty years, and her hair was long. She was the archetypal...well, all that was missing was the broomstick. Louise and I had often joked about it. She seemed friendly enough, though prone to gossip. She lifted her head as high as it would go and said "Afternoon". I smiled a hello.

She came a little closer and, uninvited, into the garden. "I'm not surprised", she said, without further explanation.

"Not surprised about what?" I wondered.

"It's because of you having that girl of yours with you."

"What, Emily?" I queried further.

"Yes, the young one. I 'spect the burglary at the church was the prompt and you having your girl here was just too much temptation for her."

I gave her a suspicious look. Then I guessed her superstitious assumption.

"So the Dutch doll got up on her wooden stumps and came to seek out my daughter at the site of her old haunts?" I asked mockingly.

"Exactly so", the old woman responded without the glimmer of a smile. "I'm probably the only one now as can remember the circumstances back in '34. And it was no laughing matter then. A young girl, a friend of mine, disappeared. That was partly what was behind the school shutting up."

"Rumour with her thousand tongues,
Makes horrid sights appear"

II

[The scene shifts to the early spring of 1934]

Winter had been particularly harsh, with a memorable blizzard that cut the village off for nearly two weeks. Now, Mother Nature was claiming back her lost children. Trees in bud and crocuses added the first dash of colour against the rust brown schoolhouse. Five girls still boarded in the long attic dormitory - twenty five others were day pupils. There was a bloodless feud between the two camps; the boarders sticking close together and defending each other, the day girls casting aspersions on the boarders' absent parents, or their "charity" status.

"Mabel Freeman is a heathen", was a popular taunt. Worse still, but only when the name callers were at a safe distance from the mistresses, was "Constance Harte, she's a tart". The other three boarders were Ethel Mann, Daisy Hazledene and Florence Dunkley. Mabel, Constance and Ethel were all eleven or twelve years old, in the senior's class. Daisy and Florrie were with the young ones. They all suffered daily jibes and tried to give as good as they got, but the insults often cut deep. The girls longed for half past four, when the day girls were set free, swinging their empty lunch bags and books tied with coarse string. Then, all five retreated to their lofty sanctuary, where they'd gossip and curse and plot.

"Miss Ozier gave me a terrible scolding today for clipping Hilda 'round the ear", said Constance. "But she deserved it, calling my dad a tramp. He's not - he's in the army, serving King and country in India." They all sat on or around Constance's bed. Bright sunlight illuminated her freckled face. Those of her friends and the other beds and furniture going towards the far gable wall, were already falling into shadow. The deep crimson curtains, plush velveteen, gave a theatrical backdrop.

"Hilda's a terrible snide", said Ethel, "we need to pay her back..."

There was a distant but firm call from the bottom of the attic stairs: "Girls, you wash up now, get ready for your tea. And Mabel, come down and start on the vegetables." All five moved almost immediately, with just enough of a pause to exchange worried looks. They were afraid of Mary Ozier.

Mary turned at the foot of the stairs, took the first floor passage leading the length of the house at the back and quickly descended the flight going down to the kitchen. There was Amy Small, laying out meat on the baking tray and sliding it into the range. The two women couldn't have been more different. Mary was in her late fifties, large, tall, with thick glasses and grey hair tied back. There was an obvious sternness about her. Amy was slight, as befit her name, and young. Her demeanour was much more open, naturally cheerful. A cheerfulness that was markedly restricted as her employer entered. For Mary was Headmistress and proprietress of the school. Her father had been a master himself, built up some fortune and, as Mary was his only child, she inherited enough to buy the school. She'd received no formal schooling, had not been to university, but had been well educated by a governess as a child and by her father in later life. Spinsterdom had perhaps not always been inevitable, but was her only life now. Amy had been employed at the school for three years. A country girl, she was being "trained up" for school mistressing, as Mary put it.

"Mabel's coming down to do the vegetables", said Mary, throwing a sideways glance at Amy.

"Please let's not..." started Amy.

"Let's not what?" Mary cut back quickly, knowing the subject matter already. "There's no use spoiling the child - spare the rod and all that. If she does wrong, if she doesn't obey, she has to face the consequences."

"But not that way", continued Amy, bravely for her, "it frightens the living daylights out of the poor creature."

"She's got to learn, they've all got to learn. Besides, you've got to instil a little bit of fear. That way you'll get respect. Molly-coddle them and you'll end up with wet good-for-nothings. Ah, there you are", Mary said, seeing Mabel standing sheepishly at the door. The headmistress quietly fetched an enamel bowl from the pantry corner. "Go and fill this with potatoes for me, there's a good girl."

"I'll get them", Amy interjected.

"No, Mabel's perfectly capable, aren't you Mabel?" Mary questioned, eyeing the girl over the rim of her glasses.

"Yes Miss", was the automatic reply, but there was trepidation there too and her eyes were wide and watering. She shuffled off towards the cellar.

"And do hurry along."

"Yes, Miss", louder this time, though still broken with suppressed anxiety.

The cellar was just beyond the kitchen, its door opposite that of the scullery in a short passage leading to the washing line and vegetable garden. Mabel clutched the bowl under one arm, because you had to turn the key that was always in the keyhole of the cellar door, at the same time as turning the latch. This done, with the door slightly ajar, she paused. "Thank heavens for electric light" she told herself, flicking on the switch and running down the stone steps. "Go straight to the potato sacks, don't turn 'round. Now fill up the bowl", quickly, with shaking hands, she did. Dropping one and realising what Miss Ozier's reaction would be to finding it later, she tutted to herself and scooped it up. She caught a very slender sight of the thing that was the focus of her fear, propped up against the far corner. "Don't look at her, don't look at her. Lord, oh Lord", she repeated to herself, in the hope that mention of the Almighty would ward off her perceived evil. Breathing fast, with every hair seemingly electrified - from her sides, the tingling feeling crept up the back of her neck to the crown of her head - she hastily finished filling the bowl. Taking the steps two at a time, she made for the door and shut it behind her, only then realising that the light was still on. So, putting the bowl on the floor and taking a deep breath, she twisted the key, turned the latch, opened the door just enough to give her thin little arm access, flicked the switch with her thumb and slammed the door with one fluid movement.

She let out a sigh of relief, picked up the potatoes, composed herself and returned to the kitchen.

"Alright, now you peel those and Amy can get started with the rest, while I lay the table", said Mary Ozier, loudly gathering up the contents of the cutlery drawer in her big hands. Mabel threw a timid smile to Amy and Amy returned a reassuring one back.

The dining table was of oak, a full ten feet long. Shining and blacked with polishing. It doubled as the needlework table for the older girls during the day, but it bore no scars; such was the care drilled into them by their mistress. Mary set the cutlery on the sideboard beyond and from the cupboard beneath, drew a snow-white tablecloth. Like casting out a fishing net, she covered the table in a single often practiced motion. Places were set for seven, with a particular deer horn handled set and a matching carving knife at the head. Oil lamps were lit, one was centred on the table and another hung by the door. After surveying the scene, she retreated to a well worn armchair in the corner, adjusted the cushion, picked up a book on the arm and settled down. She periodically kept an eye on the grandmother clock in the opposite corner. At two minutes to six, she smoothed down her ribbon bookmark, lifted herself painfully and took her place at the table. As the clock struck, Amy and the girls paraded in with crockery and serving dishes. In total silence, Mary Ozier carved the cheap pork cuts and laid out the pre-ordained ration; two slices each for the girls, three for the two women. Plates were passed clockwise, followed by the vegetables.

"Ethel, close the shutters please; there's very little light left in the day", were the only words uttered before grace. "May the Lord, in His infinite wisdom, bless all at this table. We thank Him for His bountiful gifts" and they all joined in a gloomy "Amen".

Conversation was generally restricted to three topics. Religion: solid, uncontroversial Church of England, recounting the set text of the day. Domestic: along the lines of linen, foodstuffs and the virtues of cleanliness. And the Headmistress' charmed upbringing, with stories designed to make the girls appreciate Miss Ozier's dedication to her little charges. Occasionally, when Amy and Mary discussed household business, as now, they allowed themselves harmless forays into a fourth topic: village gossip. These were latched onto with quiet enthusiasm by the girls, who relished a change from the usual dry preaching.

"Mr Gibson said he discovered some petty pilfering from his shop last Thursday", began Amy.

"Nothing that we need to be concerned about, I hope?", enquired Mary, worried and stern.

"No, no, during school hours", Amy reassured. "It seems it was the new daily help at the Mulso Arms - Mildred, I think her name is."

"Shocking", Mary mused, fishing for more detail. The girls were passing 'round the gravy boat. As it came to Mabel, she put out her hand, fingers feeling the air for china. Transfixed by the conversation, she misjudged, didn't take a firm grip and it clattered to the table. It's contents spread all the way across to the other side and dripped onto Mary's shoe.

After a sharp intake of breath among the girls, complete silence descended on the diners. Mary's face was at first shocked, then thunderous. She rose deftly and swung around to a position at Mabel's shoulder.

"Clumsy, clumsy little devil!" she hissed, taking Mabel's head at the base of her skull and pushing it forward. "See what a mess you've made, I ought to rub your nose in it." But thinking of the precious shiny surface beneath, she suddenly let go and, addressing the others, said "Strip the table, quickly, before the varnish is spoiled. And you, young lady", back to Mabel, "stand over there and not a word."

Mary stood fixed to the spot, whilst Amy and the girls busied themselves around the table. There was much noise, with Amy giving instructions. Finally, the table was bare and Amy inspected the area where the gravy was spilled. "It hardly shows at all, Miss Ozier, a quick rub with beeswax'll make it as good as new."

"Dear, oh dear", said Mary with a disgusted look at the table and an equally disgusted stare at Mabel. "What are we to do with you, my girl? You've ruined a fine piece of furniture and disrupted everyone's meal. That cannot go unpunished, now can it?" Mabel was sobbing by now, absolutely petrified. She didn't know how to answer, or even if an answer was expected, so she stayed mute, unable to say anything. Miss Ozier took her with a violent jerk of the arm, over to the armchair that was home to such a peaceful scene a short time before. She took off her right shoe, sat down and simply said "Over my knee". As she struck hard blows with the sole, Miss Ozier let loose an unbridled tirade. "May the Lord forgive you. You ungrateful little girl. If your father could see you now, he'd be utterly ashamed. Why I ever accepted you, I'll never know. You've been nothing but trouble, from beginning to end." This continued for at least twenty blows, with Mabel stifling pitiful yelps, until an imploring Amy steeled herself to say "Miss Ozier" - and Mary stopped.

"It's down to the cellar, for you my dear", Mary began, picking Mabel off her lap and leading her out into the hallway, followed by Amy. The girls were all staring at the floor, but as they were left alone, they all looked at each other with astonishment and horror, whispering "That was not fair" and "She'll not send her down again, surely."

Out in the corridor, Amy was catching up and putting a brave hand on Mary's shoulder. "The shoe was enough, Miss Ozier - and I'll make sure Mabel polishes the table 'til it gleams..."

"Not nearly enough", Mary shot back and, whispering in Amy's ear "and how dare you question my authority - you'll find yourself skivvying for farmers' wives if I let you go, so I'll hear no more." Leaving Amy trembling, Mary continued to propel the poor girl along to the feared door. Opening it and feeling some resistance from Mabel, she tugged at her arm and crouched down to face her. "Now listen here, you know what happens when your bad. Down you go until bedtime and no calling out." With that, she shoved Mabel onto the top two steps and slammed the door.

On the other side of the door, Mabel took a breath of cold air, as she heard the diminishing footsteps of her headmistress on the flagstones of the passage. Fingers fumbled in the dark for the light switch and with a heavy sigh of relief, she found it and turned it on. That feeling that she had earlier, the tingling sensation from the small of her back to the crown of her head, returned in an instant. She swivelled on her heels, keeping bal-

1 8

ance with one hand on the stair rope. She saw what she had seen a hundred times; the bare stone steps, the potato sacks, some empty crates and the edge of a large oak bookcase. The further recesses of the cellar were out of sight - you needed to be at the bottom of the steps to see the whole room. But Mabel was in no hurry to see this. Determined to last out at the top of the steps, she sat down and wrapped her grey skirt around her legs. Thoughts raced through her mind, as she tried to occupy herself. She didn't want speculation and imagination to take over. So, there was the school day and tales of darkest Africa. Mummy, as she last remembered her; sitting on the back of a cart, waving and keeping a brave face. But she could see that she was trying to hold back tears, as Mabel herself had tried to do, and failed. Happier times , in their old house, around the fire with her two smaller brothers on bath night.

These memories, good and bad, did keep Mabel calm for a while, but the cold was beginning to get to her. With no concept of time (church and school clock chimes did not reach this door), she wondered if she would ever be let out by morning. After such a long time waiting, with no shawl or blanket, the empty potato sacks looked very inviting. I'll just skip down and back up again in a matter of seconds, she thought. Unwrapping her skirts and stealing herself for a moment, she stood up, took a deep breath and went racing down. She grabbed at the two nearest empty sacks. And here's where she made her mistake. She looked up. Over in the corner, the doll stood propped up, as it was before, but this time, Mabel saw the slightest smile glide across her face. Paralysed with fear, she couldn't take her eyes off the horrid sight. Then, something that forced her to turn and run: she thought she saw the doll's left stump slide out towards her.

Dropping the sacks and flying up the steps, Mabel forgot to lift up her skirts and she trod on them. This was enough to catch her other foot and prevent it from reaching the next step. She stumbled. Shin and jaw and wrists collided with the edges of the stone steps. Yelping like an wounded animal, but still finding strength to flee from her predator, she scrambled to the top. On her knees, she bashed the door with her fists repeatedly, screaming for someone to let her out. It was then that she saw the inscription. Scratched in the door, at the very bottom, and now quite faint, were ten little words.

"Hell is the cauldron and the devil is the spoon", Mabel read out aloud. And it was then that she heard scraping, shuffling, below. She repeated louder "Hell is the cauldron and the devil is the spoon." There came rapping, rattling like a door being tried, only it wasn't the door she leant against. As she called out the phrase again and again, the rattling noise became more intense. Mabel was still frightened, she still perceived movement in the room below, but there was also a growing sense of power within her.

Just then, the cellar door opened and Mabel fell out onto Amy, who cried out at the blood on her chin, but also, Mabel thought, Amy could see something in her eyes. Amy pulled the girl away from the door, took a quick look down, turned off the light and slammed the door.

Back at the dormitory, Amy tucked Mabel up, smoothed down her hair over the off-white bandage and slipped out. The other girls waited a while and, at a given signal, they crowded around.

"You were there an awfully long time", said Mary.

"Over four hours", chimed in Ethel.

"Were you not scared?" asked little Daisy.

"There's nothing to be afraid of down there", Mabel responded, trance like. "Not as long as you know what to do."

"The windows clatter in their frames,
The doors fly open all."

III

[Forward again to 1981]

"So you were frightened by the doll as a child too - sounds like you were all....nothing short of tyrannised by your headmistress", I pondered.

"Ah, once you got to know her, there was a side you could admire", smirked Mrs Hinde, "but that's another story, for another time, maybe. I must be away now - chores to do." And without further gesture or comment, the old lady shuffled off on her stick.

I was exercising my poor arithmetic on the way over to the vicarage for tea. Already, the sky was darkening and the trees were taking on a purple tinge. A bitter wind was picking up. Nineteen thirty four, when Mabel Freeman was locked in the cellar. A school chum of Mrs Hinde. That couldn't be right. Eighty one, minus thirty four, plus eight...

"That makes Mrs Hinde about fifty five years old", I continued aloud with my musings as we sat around the vicar's table, "No, that can't be right. Perhaps Mrs Hinde was talking about a friend of her daughters?"

"I think she's childless", replied father Nick, cutting thick wedges off a flour dusted loaf. "Yes, married I heard - registry office - but no children. All before my time here, I'm afraid....and you know I don't listen to gossip."

"Of course not" I said encouragingly.

"Well, she married quite late I heard and she and her husband - he's buried in the cemetery - argued an awful lot. And at quite a volume. Caused a stir at the time, the police were called and so forth."

"She bumped him off then?", I ventured tongue in cheek.

"No, no, nothing like that", replied Nick, not getting the sarcasm. "A long, lingering illness of some sort. Then further controversy over the burial. His wife didn't come to service. Just wanted to dance on his grave, the worst of the gossips said. I wouldn't normally repeat such slander, but for the sake of the full story, you understand?" I nodded. "She never goes to church, Mrs Hinde, won't even set foot in the place. "Don't believe in that nonsense", she says to me, bold as brass. Avoids me most of the time. Took the Christmas parcel though. Come to think of it, someone else questioned her age when I put her on the list. Trying to be charitable, you know, I thought she'd welcome a parcel; she never appears very well off. As I did, add her name to the list, Mrs Amos said something about "undeserving...lamb dressed as mutton". Yes, I distinctly remembered her paraphrasing like that. I just put it down to bad feeling between the two. Anyway, she got her parcel. Snatched it out of our hands. What was the question again?"

"There wasn't one", Louise laughed, "my beloved was just puzzled about the age of the old....lady." She said, remembering that she was speaking to the vicar.

"Must be eighty", declared Nick, without hesitation.

"I hate to impose", I began, contemplating the victoria sandwich, "but are there any church records that might throw some light....?"

"You've seen the Monk's Cell, I suppose?" I shook my head. "It's above the church porch - open every flower festival; brings in a few extra coppers, you know. The parish records and a fair sized library are held in there. I'll take you over."

Sure enough, there was a slim door at the side of St Mary's main porch, with a tight spiral staircase leading to a small room, no more than eight by eight. There was a simple desk and single wooden chair in the centre and bookcases from floor to ceiling on three walls. Each one was crammed to overflowing with leather bound volumes, manuscripts and registers. All were illuminated by a harsh, bright, unshaded electric light bulb.

"A monk really did have this as is cell, did he?" I asked.

"Yes. At least up to the disillusion of the monasteries. A novice would eat, sleep and pray here. The church has accumulated these books and things over the centuries. As the dominating families of the village - the Dolbens, the Mackworths, the Pauls - died out, certain parts of their collections were bequeathed to us. But you wanted a look at the registers. Now I think Mrs Hinde's husband died in the sixties." The vicar pulled down a long grey register, dusted it off, and lay it on the table. "Luckily, there would have been no more than a funeral a week conducted here. Here's nineteen sixty. You take the left hand page and I'll take the right."

We each ran an index finger down a column of names: elaborate blue fountain pen on faded cream ruled paper. And the next page. And the next, until Nick found it.

"Here we are", he exclaimed. "Benjamin Hinde. Born 23rd of June 1915, Died - oh, again - 23rd June, 1963. Buried 25th June and then there are a couple of signatories, the vicar and a Miss C Harte. Not Mrs Hinde then. As I said, she never set foot in the church and wasn't here for the funeral. Perhaps the births will give us something. But no, drat, we of course need Mrs Hinde's maiden name for that and she wasn't married here."

"Well there's only one place to look", I said.

"Where?"

"The cemetery - they'll be something on the gravestone."

"You're not going up there now", protested Louise, as I was picking up a torch and wrapping around a scarf.

"Won't be long", I reassured, acknowledging the chiding glance with an apologetic smile. "It's only seven. I'll be back within the hour."

The cemetery was a little way out of the village, north on the station road, five minutes walk. I left my torch off and let the half moonlight and the occasional car headlight guide me between the ditches of the narrow lane. Fingers of trees met above me and the wind was making them twitch together, as though they we communicating to each other by touch. Over the bridge where the iron ore railway once rolled and into more open ground. The lights of the mill in the distance, half a mile away, were the only sign of life on this part of the desolate road. Black iron cemetery gates let out a low groan as I pushed them open. It was a sheltered spot, ringed by a tall hedge, with a row of cypresses just discernable, silhouetted black against ash to the east.

I flicked my torch on and swung its arc around. Memorials and gravestones fanned out away from the gates; the exuberance of the late Victorian and Edwardian in the foreground; giving way to grey curbed restraint and then to uniform stones, like teeth in a crowded mouth. The sixties graves would be amongst the last lot, I thought. I trod along the gravel path, trying to add weight to my confidence with the length of my strides. It wasn't working. I felt demonstrably colder and wrapped my overcoat tight to my stomach with one hand, as the other swept a blind man's stick motion with the torch. As I neared the modern graves, I though I caught a movement in the corner of my eye. Trying to dismiss it, I slowed down anyway, delaying each pace to give my hearing space. Then suddenly, what sounded like a curse, a woman spitting out vitriol.

I stopped dead. "Hello?" I said, hesitantly, then with more force "Is anybody there?" You're not at a séance, you fool, I found myself thinking. But I came back quickly with a jolt as my torchlight caught sight of a hunched figure at a grave thirty yards to my right. I stepped back one step, then thinking "come on, chicken" picked my way gradually towards the person.

"Sorry to disturb you, only I wasn't expecting anyone out her after dark. I wonder, could you help me to find…"

I was cut short as the person, the woman, shot up. She was clutching a small clear bottle, glistening with amber liquid. She shoved it into her coat pocket and gathered her clothes around her, as though she were getting changed under a towel on the beach.

"What the devil are you doing 'ere!" she snapped. It was then that I saw her as Mrs Hinde. She glanced swiftly around in all directions, worried. There was a crunch, in gravel, quite close. "Its you there is it?" the woman addressed me, gathering her composure and managing a sly smile.

"Oh, I'm dreadfully sorry, Mrs Hinde, I didn't mean to frighten you. I was just out for a walk before turning in when I spotted you." It didn't sound convincing, I knew it didn't and the old woman's smile broadened.

"Funny place to walk!" she laughed. "I was just seeing to my Ben, as is my want. He needs me more these cold nights." She picked up her stick that was leaning on the headstone. "Well, you be careful, young man. Dangerous place, the English countryside, more dangerous than you might think." She sniggered to herself and without a look back, uncharacteristically dodged spryly between the graves in the direction of the road. What was that! Something….a dog maybe…yes, maybe there was a dog waiting for her.

I shuddered audibly and cast my torch around again. The low groan of the cemetery gates could just be discerned behind me, but my torchlight did not reach that far. I waited a full minute. Listening. Nothing - except the wind high in the trees.

Turned to the grave that I was standing by, I noted that it did belong to:

A Loving Husband
Benjamin Hinde
After a long illness, bravely borne
Died 23/6/1963

No clues there then. And looking close around, it didn't look well cared for. Scraps of litter, scorched, perhaps even burnt patches of grass, and a dark green mould on the headstone. I stepped two paces to my right. Next to Hinde's grave, was Constance Harte's. The name rang a bell. Yes, the signature on the parish register against the funeral entry for Ben Hinde. The inscription here was more curious:

Rest In Peace
Constance Harte
of the Volta Tower
Tragically Killed
26th July 1963

The same summer as Ben had died. "Tragically killed" didn't sound like an easy passing either. I was convinced that I'd found something, but I didn't yet know what. I stayed long enough to repeat this second inscription ten times over to myself, so that it imprinted onto my memory. And I didn't want to stay any longer. It was very cold and I was shivering, but not just with the cold. I raced back along the path and clanked the gate shut behind me.

Marching at my swiftest pace, I headed back to the schoolhouse.

The nightmares came on again. I was in a room, in my house I perceived, with half a dozen people in it. Face-

less people who were unknown to me. But I felt comfortable and the characters in the room were talking to each
other amenably. With unimaginable speed, like a piece
of trick photography, a large dark spectre rose up behind
one of the figures in the room. I knew that this spectre
was the devil. He raised both large, claw-like hands
above his head, to the ceiling and brought them down
onto the shoulders of his victim. In the same singular
movement, he dragged this poor person down into the
ground. Although the person was not recognizable to
me, I could somehow sense the horror struck expression
on their face and could see that their breath was taken
away. Literally, their last lungful was left hanging in the
air as they were pulled down. Whispering began among
those that remained and I began to make out what they
were saying. "Hell is the cauldron and the devil is the
spoon", over and over. And I understood that this was
protection against being dragged down. Dragged down
to hell. Except that at the same time I wondered to
myself whether this was a trick that the devil was playing. That perhaps this little spell was designed to encour-
age the fiend. I felt that by saying it out loud, I was
condemning myself.

In my dream, but so clearly as to be a mouth right at
my ear, someone said simply "Four O'clock."

I jumped up and pushed the light on my beside clock.
The digital display read "4:00". Exactly. I was petrified.
Never before had a nightmare spilled into my real,
waking world. I switched on every light in the house.
Every single light. Running from room to room, illumi-
nating everything, checking behind every door, in every
cupboard. I was still scared witless and puffing like an
old grampus, when I reached the cellar door. I steeled

myself for a second, then thrust open the door. I switched on the light and charged down the stairs, growling like an animal, to give myself courage and to ward off whatever was ahead. But nothing was there. Only what I expected to find. Boxes of old toys; some wine on the shelves of the big old bookcase.

I felt relieved - all of my fears were expelled in a second. But that only lasted for a few moments. I heard a knocking sound. Three knocks, quite plain, quite clear, on what sounded like the back door. Out in the passageway, I climbed into my boots and swung my grandfathers old black overcoat over my shoulders. The back door itself was boarded up - it had lost its glass in the fire. I stood by it, apprehensive and wide eyed, waiting, listening intently. As I drew slowly towards the door, almost with my ear touching it, I began to hear whispering. A girl's voice.

At first it was indiscernible. The wind was picking up and the howling was being punctuated with bangs and crashes as debris landed. Then I gradually became able to make out the odd word: "Don't let her!...put me down there....forgotten me!" and then crying. Distant at first. Suddenly a loud scream, right next to me - in the house? - no, surely just out in the garden. I unbolted the single bolt on the back door and yanked it open. There was almost a tornado at the back of the house; the whole garden was engulfed with swirling wind and the noise was reaching crescendo pitch. In the centre was a young girl in a white nightgown, sitting on the ground, looking at me and screaming. Over her, pulling at her hair, was the Dutch doll. Just as I had seen it in the photographs, only quite animate. It seemed determined, especially after looking up and seeing me, to take the girl off. My first thought was that this girl was Emily and I strode towards them, yelling "Let her go!" Then I realised that it was not my daughter, but another girl that I did not know. But terrified, nevertheless.

I spied a shovel laying on the ground close to the couple, who were pulling each other around in a strange kind of danse-macabre. I picked it up and roared, not really intending to use it, because the girl was so close, but hoping that it would give the creature a fright. Just then, something hit me and everything went black.

When I woke up, it was much later. There was daylight, but far off. I was back inside, at the foot of the cellar steps, with the first of the morning rays cutting sharp angles through the open door above. I turned my head and gingerly felt the side, caked with a mixture of mud and blood. Making my way back into the garden, I surveyed a devastating scene. The fence on one side was down and debris littered the churned up earth. I walked over to the centre, where the disturbed ground conjured up memories from my childhood. Of cow fields by the gates where hooves left imprints in the wet mud. Here, there were round marks dotted around in a hap-hazard, manic fashion. Feeling uncomfortable, I went back into the house to telephone Louise.

"Where noises loud and dismal
Both day and night abound"

IV

[1934, the day after Mabel was locked in the cellar]

The girls woke in a subdued state - and weary after the excitement of the night before. Moving around the dormitory silently and mechanically; dressing and tidying and combing their hair. Mabel seemed set apart from this, somnambulistic almost, detached but somehow superior, smiling to herself.

Breakfast was always a less formal affair than dinner. Miss Ozier's usual absence (she often took breakfast in her room), left the borders and Amy contemplating the day ahead, over their porridge and bread and dripping, in an air of unbridled joy. In the absence of their overbearing headmistress, they could talk freely and without fear of punishment. One of the dark wooden shutters was opened and bright yellow sunshine broke in on the animated figures. Shaking the dullness from their heads, conversation drifted from confection to dresses, until one alert girl could hold out no longer and brought up again the subject dawning on them all.

"What did you learn then, Mabel, when you were locked up last night?" asked Constance.

"Learn?", replied Mabel with a touch of sarcasm, revelling in the attention that her new found courage brought her.

"Well, you said when you got back to your bed, that you weren't scared. You knew what to do, you said."

"Yes, I know all right", shot back Mabel, in ever growing confidence and scorn, "but it's a secret - I mustn't tell, or they'll be the sort of punishment that 'ud put Miss Ozier's in the shade."

"Now then Mabel", interjected Amy with a mild scold, "you mustn't speak ill of Miss Ozier - 'specially when she's done so much for you all". A muffled groan from those gathered 'round the table. But for all of Amy's initial duty to propriety, she needed some answers too. "But, did something happen to you down there? - you seemed very much affected when I let you out. And yet there was a banging beforehand."

"No, no, nothing happened really", mused Mabel, obviously thinking on her feet. "I thought I saw something, but it must have been a trick of the light. Then I fell running up the stairs - and I....I had recovered and had come to my senses when you opened the door Miss".

This satisfied the girls and they turned to something else.

"Was there anything with the doll?", whispered Amy seriously. An enigmatic smile was all that Mabel would give by return.

At "dinnertime" play, the girls were given a free rein of the yard, the garden at the rear of the school and the passageway leading to the laundry room, opposite the cellar door. The boarders helped the char-woman, old Mrs Sykes, do their laundry some days. Mabel sat on the flagstone floor, a pale and washboard between her legs, scrubbing a nightshift. Constance and Ethel manoeuvred around a washtub and mangle, with handfuls of dripping white lumps of indiscernible cloth, whilst Mrs Sykes stood hunched over the ironing board, occasionally spitting on the iron to cut into a crease. This boarder's chore was another thing that set them apart from the day pupils and, although they themselves had their own dinnertime jobs, the laundry was something that put the boarders in the "servant class". Some would be servants one day, up at The Hall, the vicarage or any one of the dozen or so "gentile" houses in the village. But a natural order placed the boarding girls and their menial tasks at the bottom of the pile. Hilda Gibson appeared at the door this time, her cutting remark rehearsed in her head:

"I have a dirty handkerchief for you Mabel, in need of a laundry-worker's scrub!" She waved the offending article with a flourish as she taunted them.

"No way to speak to your friends", cut in Mrs Sykes, sweeping her great ham-shaped forearms to and fro as she ironed, not looking up. She was oblivious to playground dynamics, to who were friend and who were enemies. Mabel and Hilda were most definitely in the latter category. Mabel forced a grimacing smile at her foe. Then her expression shifted suddenly from puzzled thought, plotting and finally to enlightened determination.

"Can I be excused Mrs Sykes?", she said, dumping her shift into the tub, "I've finished my clothes."

"Fair 'nough", muttered the woman, still not looking up, "but mind you don't get up to no good."

Mabel didn't wait for an answer, but was at the door and pulling the door to slightly. Taking three sideways steps to her left, she met Hilda, who was leaning on the opposite corner of the passageway.

"You don't scare me, Miss Freeman, Miss Heathen-Freeman", she chided with false bravery, for she was frightened underneath.

"*I* may not, but you're still afraid when it comes to the Dutch Doll", Mabel challenged.

"I'm not afraid of anything", muttered Hilda, visibly shuddering and turning her head toward the cellar door.

"I bet you daren't go down the steps", Mabel goaded, "walk over the cellar floor, *touch the doll*", (with added melodrama) "and come back up."

"You just watch me!" hissed Hilda back, with wide eyes and, with a deep breath, unlocked the door. She stood at the open doorway, hesitating.

"Go on, scaredy cat", Mabel went on, "I'll stand guard."

Hilda looked first one way along the passage, towards the kitchen and dining room, then back the other way, towards the garden and daylight, before scampering down the stairs. Mabel watched her going down; she had one hand on the door frame, the other on the open door. As Hilda left the bottom of the stairs and went out of sight to cross the cellar floor, Mabel slowly, resolutely, shut the door. As it clicked, she turned the lock and went to walk away. Just then, her friend Constance appeared.

"What are you doing?", she asked innocently.

"Nothing." was the stock bad-girl's reply.

But immediately, Hilda's muffled cries could be heard behind the closed door and it was beaten with little fists from inside. It wasn't very clear, because just at that moment the laundry was emptying of people, as they went into the garden to hang out clothes. A bucket was clanking, footsteps resonating in the corridor and mixing with girlish laughter. But Constance knew what she heard.

"You've shut someone in Mabel!"

"Don't be silly, Connie", Mabel said calmly, seizing her by the her arm and squeezing tight, making Constance wince. "Now, don't you worry about that, you just worry about what would happen if you were put down there with the Devil's own puppet, with that wooden creature scratching at you. It'll take out your eyes you know! It'll drag you down to the very pits of hell!" Mabel was hissing this out as she steered Constance out into the garden.

"And don't you tell a soul about this", she continued, "I'm just teaching someone a lesson, is all. They'll be out soon and'll know who's boss. I'm boss, alright"

"Mmmm" was all that Constance could nod, scared out of her wits.

The afternoon went quietly enough, though Constance wondered why there was no noise from the cellar. Surely, whoever was there would make such a racket at the door that someone was bound to hear?

Miss Ozier, who was taking needlecraft with the older girls, asked the whereabouts of Hilda.

"She was taken sick, Miss", piped in Mabel, who was careful to keep Constance out of earshot. "Miss Small said she should go home."

"Tut-tut, did she indeed", said Mary Ozier, looking over disapprovingly at Amy Small, who was with the globe and the little ones.

The rest of the afternoon passed uneventfully and Constance's unease was relieved when Mabel told her that she'd let Hilda out at hometime. She didn't witness it, but Mabel was perfectly convincing - and she didn't see her sly smile as she turned away. In the evening, unknown to the boarding girls, Hilda's mother came up to the school and saw Miss Ozier. She too had a suddenly mischievous edge and overlaying this with her usual over-bearing manner, soon sent the woman off with the story that Mabel had told her - that Hilda had been walked home at around one o'clock - and that she should keep a better eye on her daughter; she was obviously running everyone a merry old dance. Hilda's mother went away sobbing, saying that she'd get the men folk out to look for her when they got home.

Constance dreamt that night a compelling and disturbing dream. A girl was in the cellar - she recognised her, but in that dreamlike way, the familiarity was one step removed from the picture she was seeing. The girl in her dream was terrified - and at the top of a flight of stone steps. Constance knew the Dutch Doll when she saw it too. She had seen it on those occasions when Miss Ozier had brought it out in the daylight to show the school. The headmistress was proud of her little wooden student and posed for photographs with it on the school steps. But the doll that Constance saw in her dream was not stiff. It was animated like a dreadful automaton, marching like clockwork up the steps. And the girl who Constance recognised was crying and screaming, though no sound could be heard. An articulated hand reached around her ankle. The doll in daylight had hands carved out of a single piece of wood; this doll in the shadows had natural joints and flexibility. The girl tried to shake her foot free, which only produced a tighter grip and the doll's other hand took the girl's other ankle. Sinews and muscle seemed to strain to their limit. At the same time, the grain of the wooden hands appeared to take on more of the look of flesh and bone. In a split second, the girl's feet were lifted from under her and she was tumbling down the stairs. The doll was following her fall, still holding on to her ankles. Writhing together on the grey slabs, the girl tried to get free. To Constance at this moment, the girl's face became suddenly revealed. At first it was Hilda's, confirming her own feelings, then it was her own face. Both girls had long black hair and this resemblance was a key feature in the dream. A wind, from where she couldn't fathom, was blowing strands of black hair across the girl's face. As the face grew closer, it became clear that this was not hair at all. Hundreds, thousands of spiders were hurrying across the face. More and more, until the features were completely obliterated. Girl and doll together were swallowed up in a black hole, enveloping them as the doll clutched and pawed at it's captive.

Constance woke up. It was still dark. She gathered her sheets around her head, as we all do to give scant protection against our fears. Mabel was sitting up in the bed next to hers.

"Don't be afraid Connie", she said, "It'll not hurt you, as long as you're with me. Come on. I'll show you." Constance's bedclothes we pulled unceremoniously from her and the same vice-like grip that took her the day before, seized her again now. She wanted to scream, but the abject terror of her dream and her waking fear too, cut her mute. Mabel dragged her along the hallway at the back of the house and down the back stairs. As she was turning into the cellar door passage, she briefly loosened her grip and Constance took her chance. She took the opposite path, through the classroom and out - the front door was unlocked. There, she broke out, down into the small green below the schoolhouse. There, she began to scream, to scream out for her life.

Men were turning the corner, coming down from the church lych-gate, at the time that Constance was out on the green. There were six of them, three carrying lanterns. They had been searching the woods for Hilda. The sight of the young girl, in her white night-shift, was enough to make them jump out of her skin.

"Whoa, there!" said one, as if calming a skittish horse, "what's all this about?"

Mabel had stopped in her tracks by this stage and was retreating mindfully back into the schoolhouse.

"She's trying to get me....she's trying to get me to go down there with the doll" cried Constance.

"It's Connie Harte, is it?" asked another man. The girl nodded sheepishly. "What's bothering you? Going down where, with what doll?"

"Down into the cellar with the Dutch Doll", Constance struggled to let the words escape from her pounding chest. All the men remembered the story of the Dutch Doll and they took an uneasy look about each other.

"Now then, that's just a silly ghost story", said the first man unconvincingly, "I expect you were just having a bad dream. We'll take you back in to Miss Ozier..."

"No, no", Constance interrupted, "they'll put be down there, just like they did with Hilda!" This grabbed the men's attention.

"Hilda Dixon? Have you see her tonight? Where is she?" - the questions all came at once.

Constance looked back at the house, hesitating for a moment, then, sensing that might was on her side, said "She put Hilda in the cellar today!"

"What!" said one.

"Come on, we must have it out with the school ma'am" said another. "We've been up searching half the night. If that woman's got her all along, they'll be hell to pay" and three of the men strode up to the door.

"Best get the constable first", said one of those remaining on the grass with Constance. Seeing PC Bankes coming down Bell Hill, the man thought quickly and added "and perhaps the parson too". He headed back up to the church, shouting across to the policeman: "They think she's in the schoolhouse Harry - I'm going to get the vicar."

"Right O, Frank", replied the PC, striding determinedly onto the scene.

The Police Constable, the five remaining search party members and a bewildered and feared Constance climbed the steps to the pavement, through the iron gates and up to the wide door of the girl's school. It was a cool, damp night, the air was perfectly still and the moon was half full. The light it cast, when it parted purple clouds, made the tarmac shine on the road below and gave the ironstone house a deep red colour. The front door was ajar. Sitting in the hallway were Mabel in her nightgown and Mary Ozier, fully dressed. The headmistress had her hand on the shoulder of her charge and was whispering to her.

"Is that you, Miss Ozier", PC Bankes ventured.

"Yes it is, Henry Bankes - and most annoyed too. What on earth has got into you and your men - scaring the living daylights out of my girls? And at this hour!"

"We don't mean to disturb you or yours Miss, but we've been up 'til this hour searching for Hilda Dixon."

"That's no business of mine. What that young mischief maker gets up to outside school is the business of her parents", Mary Ozier retorted.

"Except now, Miss, this young girl….Connie Harte", said PC Bankes, revealing the shivering girl behind him in the shelter of the men, "she tells us she reckons Hilda is in your cellar."

A shocked Mary Ozier tried to recover her resolve: "Absolute nonsense", she said beckoning, "and come on in Constance, you'll catch your death."

"Sorry Miss", muttered Constance, taking hesitant and seemingly precipitous steps towards her teacher, "but Mabel told me that…", then she cut herself short and retreated a step or two, remembering who she was speaking to; what the threat of punishment was.

"Never mind that - come on in" repeated Miss Ozier in ominous staccato.

"We do at least need to look about your lower floors", proceeded the PC, mustering his best courtroom English, "owing to the seriousness of the occasion and potential danger to a young child's person." The men behind the policeman were grumbling by this time and growing more and more impatient.

"Come on lads, we'll not be left hanging on here, surely", one said and they all muttered approval, "Let's get in then!" and against a torrent of loud objections from Miss Ozier and Mabel, they barged their way in. The men were having no nonsense once inside and, turning on the few electric lights, searched the classrooms and dining room, the sound of shifting furniture and breaking glass punctuating the policeman's continuing remonstrations with Miss Ozier out in the hallway.

"Here's the cellar door Harry...you going down?" shouted one man from the back.

"Perhaps I can be of help?", came the mild voice of the parson, Reverend Samuel Paul, as he entered the open front door. He was wearing his wellington boots and a raincoat over his pyjamas. Rev. Paul came from a long line of vicars of this parish and appeared to have evolved into his shape: tall, wiry and hunched, with thinning hair, a long bird-beak nose and wire rimmed spectacles.

"Ah, Reverend, at last someone to bring reason to this riot - kindly tell these *people* to leave the schoolhouse; they're frightening my girls." Mary Ozier was clutching at straws. She and the vicar did not get on; Miss Ozier outwardly the dutiful Christian woman, inwardly nursing a deep resentment against the parson. This resentment did not go unnoticed by the Rev. Paul.

"Of course, I'll try and calm things down Miss Ozier", in a quiet undertone to the headmistress, then in firm measured tones to the men into the passageway: "Gentlemen, I'm sure we can settle this without any more fuss."

"They've got Hilda down 'ere vicar", protested one.

"Yes, Tom has told me" and to Miss Ozier, "we'd better have a look to satisfy the search party and the constable."

"There's no need, I've told you - she's not here", Miss Ozier reiterated, clearly agitated.

"I really must insist, Miss", the PC went on, following the men into the passageway. Then cries of "look at this here" and "there's blood on the steps" and "watch where you're stepping". Miss Ozier turning paler by the second back in the hallway and Mabel looking to her in vane for reassurance. Finally, a shout of "Vicar, can you come down here please", from the constable.

The Reverend took slow wary steps down into the cellar. There was blood on the steps and drops of it on the flagstones and the Dutch Doll, lying on the floor, with more blood on her face. No girl to be seen.

"I need to go and telephone the station", said PC Bankes. As he took a couple of steps back up, the vicar saw something that perturbed him greatly.

"Wait a while, Harry", rasped the reverend, "Oh Lord, protect us!"

"What's the matter sir?"

"We need to move this doll - its an abomination! We need to move it...into the church. Yes." And leaning down to the wooden face, hissed "Get thee behind me, Satan!" Two men helped him carry the doll to the church, under fierce protests from Miss Ozier. Eventually, she returned back down the hill to the school, grumbling and weeping weakly into her coat. The Rev. Paul stayed in the church the two hours 'til dawn, insisting that the men kept with him and, at the cock's crow, sent one away for the blacksmith.

"The women cry -
The men go pale with fear"

V

[1981, the day after my own nightmare]

I said I'd meet Louise in the church. Away from both Nick, our vicar - Louise had told me that he'd been called to the bedside of a sick parishioner - and away from our daughter, who was impressionable and likely to get agitated by any recounting of my story in her presence. I was alarmed enough for all of us, as I toyed with the loose mortar and holes in the stonework, where the Dutch Doll had once been shackled to the back wall of the church. Everything else in the church seemed in its right place and unthreatening: the flowers arranged by the font; the book of remembrance carefully opened at today's date, under the roll of honour; the flames of three small votive candles flickering in their place near the pulpit.

Louise arrived and I felt instantly relieved. I held her longer and more tightly than usual. "Are you OK? You sounded quite shocked on the phone and I wondered…" she paused as I winced when her fingers swept through my hair, then her eyes widened, "hey, are you hurt - what's this?" inspecting more closely the cut in my scalp above my ear.

I explained, as I recalled, all that had happened the night before. The names on the gravestones in the churchyard. How I'd found Mrs Hinde apparently in the middle of a ritual at her late husband's spot. My dreams and their all-too-real climax.

"Hallucinations, surely?" Louise tried to reason, "you've worked yourself up, got yourself spooked by these stories and they're coming alive in your dreams."

"And this?", I gestured at my wound.

"You must have been sleepwalking and fell over."

"Have you ever known me to sleepwalk?"

"No...."

"And there's definitely something connecting old Mrs Hinde to all this" I proffered.

"The witch, you mean?", Louise smiled light-heartedly.

"Yes. Her husband died and the woman that attended his funeral, signed in the parish register, died a few weeks later, "tragically", the inscription reads."

"So there's a twenty year old mystery, that may not be a mystery at all - and its giving you nightmares. I really want to be sympathetic, but its hard, you know?" I smiled weakly. "Perhaps you'd better stay at the vicarage with us for the next couple of nights. The house can look after itself. The repair work and redecoration are all scheduled for the next day or two, then we can all move back in together. OK?"

"I suppose..." I shrugged.

With Emily ensconced at her aunt's, we had a couple of hours to take lunch at the Bell Inn. It is a very old pub, remodelled in high gothic; still in the rich brown ironstone that constituted all the buildings around the church. I couldn't shake the shadow of my all consuming topic and broached the subject to the landlord at the bar.

"Tom, were you here in the sixties? Would you know anything about a Constance Harte, who died in 1963?" Tom screwed up his well worn brown face in pained puzzlement, before shaking his head.

"No, a bit before my time; but I know a man who might - George, over there by the fire, he's the local historian, knows most about anything."

I thanked the landlord and sauntered over. "Excuse me...George?" The old man, with pipe and horn rimmed glasses, who until then was lost in the licking flames of the hearth, turned surprised for a moment, then nodded with raised eyebrows. "Tom said that you were quite an authority on local history."

"Well yes, I've gathered together a few old photographs and newspaper cuttings, scribbled a few lines, for the local paper, things like that. What's your interest?"

"I wondered if you knew how Constance Harte came to die?"

"Yes", George drew out the affirmation slowly, looking troubled and dropping his eyes, "I more than know about it, I was at the scene. I was a member of the local fire brigade. The village had a part time volunteer service at that time and a small engine. One fine summer's day, the Volta Tower - you'd heard she lived in the Volta Tower - well it collapsed around her. She didn't stand a chance. Tons of rubble we had to shift, before we came across her..."

"What was the Volta Tower like - surely it couldn't just have fallen down?"

"It was...there's a picture of it on that wall there look," I studied a sepia photograph as he continued, "it was made of dry stone, little or no mortar and top heavy. They say that the temperature that day must've contributed. Though it had stood for nigh on two hundred years. Remarkable building in many ways. Built by Sir Thomas Dolben, to commemorate his son, who died in a shipwreck. The ship was called the Volta."

"That's very enlightening, thank you." I took the opportunity to ask one more thing: "And are you familiar with the story of the Dutch Doll?"

"Yes, but I'd advise you not to dig too deep there. It's a bit of an unmentionable subject among most folks that can remember it. It being stolen will rake it all up again. You the one as lives at the old girl's school?" I nodded. "Mmmm, so you'll know about the passages? No? They say that there are passages underground between the church and your house and this pub. I suppose built as bolt holes during the persecution of the Catholics; but the vicar will be able to enlighten you about those. The Dolben crypt is supposed to be the starting point for one end. As far as the doll goes, by all means I can try and fill you in, but you're better off letting sleeping dogs lie. I had a brush..." and he stopped, considering it wise to stay dumb.

"I would like to clear one or two things up in my mind, if I could? But I have to get back to my wife just now". He gave me his address and we parted happily enough; though he was eying me warily.

"Where have you been?" asked Louise as I returned to our table.

"Just chatting to that old man", I hesitated, then smiled, "about my old obsession. He's just enlightened me about several aspects of the story..."

Later, I was moving some of my things to stay in the vicarage. Nick had kindly agreed to extending his hospitality to my whole family. Close enough to our house for me to keep an eye on the repair work. I found Nick in his study, pouring over a map.

"You said that George Mason was telling you about passages. It did ring a bell and I unearthed this map in the church library. George was right, there were tunnels, or at least tunnels marked with question marks - so at the time this map was drawn, in the 1850's, their exact whereabouts wasn't certain, but all do seem to converge on the church - on the east end, at the Dolben crypt. We let people have a peep, even step down into the main chamber - on fete days. But no one has gone beyond the grate (there's a black grill that would take you down into a deeper cavity) for years."

We looked seriously at each other for a long ten seconds.

"Are you thinking what I'm thinking?" Nick ventured in the end.

"I think so", I said.

"I doubt the Bishop would approve, but it would not be desecration, in fact I could say a prayer for the departed souls whilst we're there. It could be a strengthening - re-consecration if you like - particularly if there has been a sinister link between your house and the church." Nick was obviously trying to talk himself into investigating the crypt, and I wasn't about to stop him. But I did say:

"No one has said that the link, the tunnel if there is one, is sinister. George said it was probably a source of refuge."

"I'm uneasy, but I am drawn to it. I feel that there has been a disturbance and that the church is somehow under attack. And it's my job to protect against such evil attacks" I wanted to laugh at this, but I could see that Nick was deadly serious. "No time like the present. I'll need my bible and I'll need to get my torch from the garage. Meet me 'round by the East end of the church in ten minutes. You'll need to bring the ladder. It's in the shed at the back."

The evening was drawing in as I stood there by the crypt entrance, trying to peer down into the darkening void. Some light was suddenly shed as the church lights came on and threw a dim Christmas-tree-like illumination on the proceedings. I was shivering - there would be a frost that night, but that wasn't it. Presently, Nick turned the corner with a torch in one hand and a box of candles in the other.

"The battery's not that great, so we may need to revert to the traditional method", he said smiling bravely. He fumbled in his pockets for matches, handing them to me, and for the key, a large solid iron thing. "Now, there's a knack to this." He shook the key in the monstrous lock, which looked like the body of a black crab. With a deft twist, it freed itself and the lock came apart, wriggling from the two wrought iron gates as they swung inwards. "Let's have the ladder down". I gingerly lowered the ladder down, until it came upon solid stone. "You see, it must only be eight feet down to the first part", said Nick.

Without waiting for the "who's going first" debate, I began to descend the ladder, as Nick held the dimming torch to where my feet were going. After counting twelve steps, they rested on expensive Portland stone and, even without great illumination, I could see, could feel almost, the creamy white polishedness of the small hole into which I'd dropped. I held the bottom of the ladder as Nick came down after me. He said, "Let's light a candle or two", as he came to my level. I obliged with the matches and we each held a candle. Nick produced his gardening gloves and we put on one apiece to protect ourselves from the dropping wax. A neat little candle-holder was the essential item of a century before - we made do. The pale gentle light that filled the chamber showed human sized receptacles at eye level, some occupied and sealed with engraved plaques, others empty cavities, waiting for family decedents that never appeared.

"The last of the Dolbens was Eleanor who died in 1910 - here she rests" said Nick, moving his candle towards one inscription. We were both drawn towards the black grate in the floor, a close square mesh made of half inch thick lengths of iron, measuring perhaps four feet by three. "Let's see if we can move this", motioned Nick. We could see through the grill that coffins were piled up below. They looked as though they were just made of card, the wood perishing. Some had lids that were caving in, others with their indiscernible contents exposed. We both dripped a little wax and planted candles to the side, then slipped fingers through the grill at one end.

I said "After three" and counted "one, two and three" and with all the strength we could muster, heaved at the grate. It came up remarkably easily, not corroded, not fused with its frame. But very heavy. It took our combined efforts to lever it on its side and over, as gently as we could, onto the floor. "We'll need the ladder again". We lowered, about the same depth again, into the darker lower chamber.

This time Nick said "My turn, I think" and went down first, but he was saying a prayer to himself. "Lord protect us and bring us both through this journey..." was all I heard as he descended. Then, after a pause and some shuffling, he said, "Everything's alright; come down." I followed the vicar into the deep crypt. The lower chamber was of the same dimensions as the upper one, about twelve feet square, but had no receptacles for coffins in the walls, the chamber itself was stacked full of them. There were about twenty in all. Three columns of 5 or 6 coffins each, neatly piled on top of each other, two small ones in one corner and one adult casket, on it's side and with the lid seemingly prised off.

"It looks like its been defiled by someone", said Nick.

"There's a small brass plaque on that piece", I pointed, then read "Thomas Dolben, 1752 - 1778. He didn't live long, but then I suppose life expectancy wasn't up to much in those days."

"He was the Thomas Dolben, eldest son of the Dolben, also called Thomas, who built so many things around town; this crypt, your girl's school, remodelled the Bell Inn and so on." explained Nick. "But this Thomas Dolben - Junior - was the one brought back from the West African coast, who died in the shipwreck."

"And in building the crypt, Sir Thomas Dolben - Senior - came across the tunnels", I said, turning my attention to another, smaller grill against the wall by the children's coffins. I approached it gingerly and could feel a draught of air from it.

"Maybe", said Nick, "But first, I'd like if I may, to say that prayer for this young man and his family here around us." I bowed my head, more distracted than I should have been, keeping one eye on the grate I'd just spotted.

"Lord Jesus, I'm certain that our brother here, Thomas, and the many members of his family that surround him are known to you. May their souls be at peace, may their sins be forgiven and may they be at your father's feet. I pray, Lord, that you are with them and they are with you. Preserve and protect them, oh Lord, for in you they put their trust. Amen"

"Amen", I repeated and turned, perhaps with undue haste, to the grill. Raising my flickering candle to it, I could see stone walls beyond, making way to rougher bricks, but another chamber, or passageway, definitely lay beyond. "Shall we see if this will move as easily as the first one?" I asked, clawing at it eagerly, though with fast beating heart. It did shift slightly and a fine dust carried on the draught and smudged my coat. "The two of us should do it", I offered. Nick came to my aid and the grate did give way. This one, being vertical, was hinged. It swung out towards us, uttering a disagreeable deep moan. I put my candlelit arm into the hole and, yes, sure enough, a narrow passage headed off to the south east, away from the church. The walls were constructed of rough brickwork, arched at the top and about five feet above the dirt floor. I crawled through the entrance first and stood up, as far as I could. Nick came in behind me.

"It is what we thought then", said Nick.

"Yes and open at the other end, or we wouldn't feel the breeze. We must count our paces and try to map out

in our heads, whereabouts we are in relation to the surface features." I counted seventy paces, along rubble
strewn but otherwise rubbish free tunnel to about where
the road would be, before we reached a junction. At
that point, there was a cross road. A broken lantern,
some old newspapers, with 1930s dates and pieces of
wood marked the dissection. One passage to our left,
only went on for few yards, before it was apparently
blocked by debris and piping. "A sewerage pipe?", I
guessed. To our right and straight ahead, lay tunnels
similar to the one we had just traversed. I paused and
licked a finger.

"This one", I pointed ahead, "is the one that is open
to the air." We crept, stooping, along for another 25
paces until the tunnel curved to the right and then
dramatically narrowed and shortened. We could start to
hear the sound of running water. I crawled until I
reached an opening, barely two foot square, where it met
another wider tunnel at right angles to it. My head was
high up in the adjoining passage, and a subterranean
steam ran swiftly from left to right. "This must be the
river that used to run through the village", I shouted
back to Nick, remembering that a couple of the roads
"up stream" were called "Affleck Bridge" and "Water-
low Bridge".

"Nothing else here", I said, edging back on my hands
and knees, "Let's try that other one." We retraced our
steps, back to the junction of the four tunnels, then along
the one we originally saw to the right. This one snaked
and inclined upwards, until we reached a rough timber
door. "I reckon we're about at the Bell Inn", said Nick.
The clay and glass bottles strewn about this branch of the
tunnel could have led us to the same conclusion. He

rattled the door. Dust flew up and swirled around us. This was a dead end as far as fresh air was concerned. There were splits in the wood of the door, big enough to slip a finger through. Something hard and cold was right up against the other side of the door. "I think it's bricked up", Nick said.

We moved back towards the intersection again, snaking down. As we did, before we took the final turn to the junction itself, there was a distinct, audible exhalation, a cross between a heavy sigh and a growl, a clanging sound and running steps. Nick and I stopped in our tracks, for just two seconds, before I shouted "Who's there, what are you doing down here!", by which time I'd taken the few steps back to the crossroads. Nothing, except the same lantern, upturned this time and the sound of running steps disappearing into the distant echoes of the passage to the crypt.

"Some boy from the village", Nick suggested.

"Damn fool! What on earth is he doing down here", then shouting ahead of me, "hey, come back, we won't hurt you!" All the time, we were making our way as fast as we could back towards the crypt entrance, candlelight shifting from bright illumination to pitch black as we swung our arms, heads hunched against the tunnel arch. Then we heard a loud clang.

"He shut the bloody gate - Hey!" I shouted as we reached the grill, which, as I thought, was what made the noise. "Come back here!" I screamed in rasping anger. I just caught sight of a foot (*no, not a foot*), leaving the lower chamber. More footsteps, then silence. Nick and I were both gasping, in fear and through exertion.

"I think it was the doll!" I exclaimed, too shocked for censorship of the apparently impossible.

"The Dutch Doll?", Nick asked, without expecting an answer, "well, we must get out and hunt it down", he added with surprising understanding.

"So...so you believe me?" I asked.

"I've told you before, if one believes in God, one must believe in the evil one and he has many of his own disciples." He began pushing at the grate, "we must get out of here and do something." What to do, I'm sure had not moulded properly in Nick's mind. Neither had I got it in mind firmly, but a mixture of concern for my own family and a need to contain, destroy, kill, this creature that I'd seen in my living nightmare.

We took turns to barge at the grill with our shoulders, an awkward business, as it was low down at the tunnel exit. Then it was kicked and finally we both tried to exert a sustained pressure on the iron. Without success. It was definitely fixed more firmly than when we entered through it. We gave way to shouting, as loud as we could, first with ad hoc pleas, then with orchestrated cries of "help" and "in the church". After what seemed like an age, but what was in fact just 10 minutes, someone finally approached.

"Is that you vicar?", it was Betty Underwood, who lived in Hampton Cell, a small cottage just by the church gate. She'd heard us from her garden.

"Yes, bless you Betty", replied the vicar, "we're trapped down here - please fetch some help to get us out."

"Straight away vicar", we heard back.

"Be careful out there....", Nick trailed off, realising that she was on her way. "Though I don't think you know, that the doll, if the doll is up there and *at large*, is a real threat to us. It may be a possessed entity perhaps, but we've only seen that it was involved in a car crash when it was stolen - the speed of the getaway and nerves could have brought that about. Otherwise it has only come to you in dreams."

"I hate to admit it, for fear of sounding foolish, only I felt that they were not dreams, that I was wholly awake and aware at certain times. I'd like to share your optimism about the limit of the doll's influence. But I really feel afraid that it is far more dangerous than you think."

Two men shouted down at that moment; they'd been accosted by Betty Underwood on their way to the pub. Presently we heard, with much muffled cursing, them dropping down into the upper chamber of the crypt and down the ladder into the lower one. "What on earth are you doing in there vicar?" one asked incredulously. He and his friend pulled hard at the grate, as we pushed from inside the tunnel. It gave way suddenly, then swung open with ease. We gave lame answers to the questions the men posed, but insisted that we all get to the surface post haste. Coming over the edge of the top chamber and catching the welcome sight of streetlamps, I was greeted by the dreadful sound of my wife screaming. I sprinted around the church, back into the vicarage garden, where Louise was frantically searching through the bushes.

"Emily, Emily!", she was crying. And to me: "She's gone - I thought that she'd settled down and I was just going in to kiss her goodnight and she was gone. Not in her room, not in the bathroom. Nowhere in the house." She was sobbing uncontrollably as I ran to the rear of the vicarage, shouting frantically for my daughter.

"And if the spectre should appear,
Their work they will let fall"

VI

[Beginning in the early hours, the next day, 1981]

Louise was told the whole story, as much as was familiar to us, at 4am, as we sat around the vicar's kitchen table. Nick was calm and under control, more than Louise and I could possibly be under the circumstances. We had called the police at about eleven, after frantic searching of the vicarage and its outbuildings, the gardens, those of our nearest neighbours and the church and churchyard. Nothing. Then the police swung into action, pretty professionally, thinking back. They set up base in the vicar's study, mustered fifteen officers and countless local volunteers and widened the search. But only in the village houses and gardens. The Inspector in charge, Vines his name was, was unwilling to venture out into the countryside.

"Plenty of time for that in the morning - and we'd do a far better job of it then", Vines said, adjusting his trousers around his ample waist. "Besides, we don't suspect anything...serious at this stage. More often than not, in these cases, the missing child turns up with a relative or friend, or asleep in a coal bunker and has come to no harm."

Of course, we had not told the police everything. Any hint of hocus-pocus would ruin our credibility from the outset, we realised. Instead, we tried our best to rule out the innocent theories as to Emily's whereabouts and vocalise our fears. Our fears were real enough and Vines was convinced of the dangers (albeit unspecified) that we considered our daughter to be in.

So, after all that could be done in the first few hours *had* been done, Nick made us a cup of tea and convened a private council in the kitchen.

"Yes, absolutely the right thing, not going the whole hog", Nick was saying, "The moment we bring in the supernatural, we have the devil of a job trying to get the police to take us seriously again."

"We really must get out there, if Emily has gone, has been taken by something", said Louise, tear-stained and shaky, but resolute and determined.

"Yes, but we can't just disappear...", I added.

After a seconds thought, Nick said "I'll just tell Vines that I'm taking you around to your mother's house."

Five minutes later we'd stopped Nick's Landrover on the Harrowden Road, near to the site of the thieves' accident and out of site of the last policeman, who was pacing the road back and forth, stamping his feet against the cold.

"We must, absolutely must, stick together - all three of us. First," Nick said, emphasising the importance of what he was saying, "first, it prevents any one of us from getting lost or in trouble. Second, if we do see anything, we *all* see it. Understand?" And he wouldn't let us move on until he had our word.

A hard frost made the going along the side of the field easy and the clear sky made full advantage of the pale moonlight. We headed for the spinney and the Holly Walk, talking in whispers.

"We can double back on ourselves and head back towards the vicarage, through the wood and along the Walk", Nick suggested. Leading from the old Hall to the West was a promenade of holly trees, planted a hundred and fifty years before and now much overgrown, but still navigable. This was the Holly Walk. The Old Hall itself was abandoned and ramshackled, fought over by developers, though no scheme had ever come to fruition.

First, we entered the spinney at its lower end. A path cut through it from top to bottom, but this was quite indiscernible in the dark, Nick's fading torch our only source of artificial light. Moonlight penetrated tendriled fingers of the branches above somewhat. I could barely see my feet, which added to my feelings of unease. We talked in whispers and decided to take ten paces at a time, stopping at these intervals to shout Emily's name - to shout moderately, not bellowing, as we were aware that the police were posted around the village and would disapprove of our amateur, clodhopping search. Loud enough though, to reach to the edge of the spinney as we walked up through it. After our call, we would stand still, count ten seconds to ourselves, listening, then move forward another ten paces. In this way, we traversed the whole of the wooded area, some 300 yards long. I felt a black dog following me; whether imaginary, of the sort that have haunted poor demented souls for hundreds of years, or real, a sinister creature tracking us in the shadows, I couldn't tell. I couldn't share this feeling, this dreaded encircling, with the others, though I felt it sure enough.

Coming out of the wood was like stepping out into the daylight - and perhaps there was a hint of dawn to the east. The Holly Walk stretched out in front of us, overgrown and dilapidated, but still plainly an avenue of holly trees, the parallel rows fifteen yards apart. We continued our routine as before, pacing through the fallen leaves, speaking out Emily's name and listening. Repeating this sequence eight or nine times, we stood to discuss options.

"We're about 250 yards from the end of the Walk, then there's the Hall grounds, then the vicarage, so we'll come across a police sentry somewhere around the Hall", I supposed.

"There's the old quarry railway line off that way", gestured Louise to her left.

"We'll try that, then head back", I said, "maybe there'll be some news back at the vicarage..."

Two figures appeared instantaneously at the far end of the walk. An adult and a child. You could hear our sudden intake of breath.

"Hey!", Louise shouted instinctively, but it was probably the worse thing she could have done. The two figures stood stock still, then both ran into the woods. Strange, I thought, that if that was Emily, what would she be doing running off with someone, not taken or dragged. Unless it was someone she knew and she was happy to go. We ran as far as we could towards the spot where they had run off. On the way, Nick stumbled and fell, urging us to carry on. The Ice Tower loomed up at the side of the Walk. I'd forgotten about this. It was used as a giant freezer by the Hall when it was occupied - filled with ice to preserve meat. Almost as much of its internal space went underground as we could see projected above it. We reached the spot by the Ice Tower where the two had decamped into the trees, out towards the abandoned railway line.

"You stay here." I said to Louise "I can travel quicker on my own."

"But Nick said we should stick together."

"Never mind that now - anyway the sun's almost up - I'll meet you back at the vicarage by the time the church clock strikes six."

I ran as fast as I could through the trees towards the railway line. My breath was heavy and visible, trailing behind me like a steam train. I was afraid but driven with a strong sense of indignation and anger. No one was going to take my girl and get away with it! I suddenly came upon the cutting. In fact it took me by surprise and I slid down the earth bank. I quickly gained my footing and looked in both directions. Nothing to the left and....yes, to the right, the two figures again, this time hand in hand making their way along the line. I bounded after them. The track had been taken up, concrete sleepers remained. Leaping from sleeper to sleeper, I built up momentum. Gaining on the two figures ahead of me, I pressed on, then saw them scramble up the bank by the bridge. It must have been where the Station Road passed over the line. I reached the same point in the bank and scaled it with the boundless energy that adrenalin brings. Clawing my way through the hedge at the top, ripping my cheek in the process, I came onto the road. At first I thought the road was empty, then I saw the Dutch Doll, unmistakably the Dutch Doll, retreating backwards through the hedgerow on the other side. Its cold eyes and face betrayed a satisfied malevolence - it looked me right in the eye, raised a hand as if to point at me and disappeared. This all happened in a second. At the same time, I realised that someone was to my side; I heard someone trying to catch their breath. Turning, I saw Mrs Hinde, holding her chest, drawing in the cold air with a pained expression. The sun was rising, tingeing the old woman's face orange.

"What are you doing here?", I asked directly, "was that you on the line?"

"Me? Down there? , oh no" she defended herself, "I was just coming up from my house...looking for your girl." Seeing my incredulous look, she changed her tack and her expression, spitting forth:

"Don't you go messin' about my business anymore! You need to mind your own business and not go meddlin' in things that you don't understand. You're an outsider here - stay outside. Stay clear of village matters!"

"I want to find my daughter, nothing else", I said, my anger rising, "and you know something about it - you and your..." pointing at the far hedgerow, "..your accomplice. I've seen the Dutch Doll now, in near daylight, fully conscious, with my senses unimpaired. I know it exists and that it moves about - moves about with you!" I was approaching her now, "Tell me where my daughter is, now!"

At first, Mrs Hinde drew back, afraid, then her confidence appeared to return suddenly. An awful stench arose, like rotting flesh. Not just this, but another unseen repellent forced me away from her.

"You can't touch me", she said defiantly, "No, you'll not harm me, nor my friend." And she was gone, retreating through the same hedge as the Dutch Doll. I was desperate to follow, if my legs could move. They remained leaden, until I turned finally back down the road to the church, remembering my six o'clock promise.

I got back to the vicarage to find the police vans packing up and driving away - and Inspector Vines on the doorstep talking to the vicar.

"We found her - she was in the Ice Tower", said Nick.

"Talking some nonsense about the Dutch Doll. Of course, we're still investigating that theft. The vicar here was just telling me about the local superstitions", Nick and I exchanged knowing looks, as Vines went on: "obviously Emily has been imagining things. I think we can put this down to nocturnal wanderings. She presumably found shelter in the Ice Tower and fell asleep. Still, all's well that ends well, we won't need to impose on your hospitality any longer vicar…" Already, I was passing the two men and heading to the study, where I could hear Emily & Louise talking. After ardent and desperate embraces, I settled down to listen to Emily's story.

"There was, like, a puppet in my room and she took me out of the house", she began. "She was quite nice at the start, but she did pull me along hard. Said she had something secret to show me. Then we came to the Ice Tower and I think I was pushed down into it, because I woke up inside, with the puppet and someone else - a grown up - standing by me. Then the thing started scratching at my legs and I didn't like it and I started screaming. And Mum and Nick came to rescue me."

"She does have scratch marks around both ankles", Louise showed me.

"My God", I said "and did the doll, the puppet, say anything to you? What did it sound like?"

"Just like a little girl", Emily replied, "she said she'd teach me a rhyme to make me less afraid. But she didn't get round to it."

"I've dreamt about a rhyme myself", I said quietly to Louise, "I think I remember it, but I'm not sure that its safe to utter - it feels like a spell or a curse. Dangerous."

After we all caught up with some sleep, I settled Louise and Emily with Louise's parents for a few hours, whilst I paid a visit to local historian George Mason.

George lived in a small flat above the bakers in the High Street. It had an inauspicious entrance and stairway, drab with peeling paintwork. He welcomed me with what sounded like oft repeated apologies for the clutter. 'Clutter' was an understatement. Barely a square foot of furniture, wall or floor-space was left unoccupied. Papers were strewn everywhere; newspapers, books, magazines, maps, photographs and postcards - as though a sack full of ephemera had been emptied out in front of strong electric fan. Bookcases lined the wall, with the wall over the fireplace taken up by a dim and dirty Victorian 'stag at bay' picture framed in overly elaborate gilt-work. There was a desk, a lamp and two easy chairs on either side of the lit fire. George cleared these seats and offered me one.

"I hear that you were bothered further last night", he opened, not beating about the bush. "Your daughter wander off?" he asked, I realised, hopefully.

"No, I'm afraid not wandering, although that's what the police have swallowed, because what I think to be the truth would not be palatable to them at all."

"Mmmm, I see", meditated George for a moment, "then you'll not be unfamiliar with the worst kept secret in town. Those of us brought up in the village in the thirties will remember the last disturbances. Most of us don't care to bring it to the forefront of our minds and time, besides being a great healer, also dulls the memory. And we're rather embarrassed to even bring up the topic, as I am skirting around it now, because these days it is faintly ridiculous. The Dutch Doll I'm of course alluding to. With a life of its' own and it being possessed I mean. There, I've said it - out in the open now. If you have a different story to relate, if your recent troubles are down to something logical and tied to the earth, then laugh at me now and I'll go no further."

"No, no, I'm not about to laugh, not by any means. Like you, I can scarcely bring myself to express out loud what seems too fantastic. You see, I believe my daughter to have been abducted by the doll last night. I've been having vivid dreams concerning the doll for the last few nights and this morning I saw it moving, looking at me, as clear as day, almost as close as you are to me. And that's not all, I know who's controlling the doll, or colluding with it at least - Mrs Hinde.

George looked suddenly devastated, but not surprised. "Those two have linked up already then. I was afraid they would, but I was hoping that the doll had been carried away, far away - and that the nightmare, if it had to be visited on anyone, would afflict another person, another community." He then outlined the story of the disturbances before the second world war, Miss Ozier's attachment, the disappearance of a girl, what he called "the apprenticeship, the recruitment" of another schoolgirl.

"And that girl grew up to be Mrs Hinde?" I asked.

"Yes. Mabel Hinde - Mabel Freeman as was. A sweet little girl at one stage, I remembered, but ever since that episode - well, nothing short of poisonous."

"But she stayed in the village, even married?"

"Stayed, yes. Things died down eventually and, well, you can't try anyone for witchcraft in the twentieth century. Married an outsider. A union soon regretted and soon ended. Not in altogether innocent a manner either. Though again, those of us that had suspicions, didn't have the nerve to confront her, or the gall to go to the authorities."

"So what happened?"

"As I said, married an outsider, Ben Hinde. Mabel met him when she was doing war work, a munitions factory in Coventry, I think. When she moved back to the village towards the end of the war, he tagged along, getting a boot & shoe job at the main road. They married soon after - registry office - and settled into one of the new prefabs. If settled is the word. Continually rowing they were, quite notorious for it. She built up a reputation as a back-street abortionist and apothecary, grew very old and bedraggled looking very quickly. He spent more and more time down the pub, until he became ill. His was a slow, creeping death. First, he just appeared very tired and grew black, sunken eyes. Next, a numbness of his limbs set in. Lastly he became housebound, where he could be heard from the street, groaning. Mabel wouldn't let anyone else attend to him. The Police were eventually called by a brave neighbour and broke into the house, but it was too late. The doctors could find nothing physically wrong, besides a form of anaemia and despite having a blood transfusion, he died within a week."

"Mrs Hinde didn't attend the funeral, the vicar tells me?" I fished.

"Wouldn't, couldn't almost, attend church at all. Had an intense dislike for church and churchgoers - bunch of no good do gooders, she'd say. Stayed clear on the day of the funeral. Wasn't even at the cemetery for the internment."

"I'm intrigued also by this death at the Volta Tower. Constance Harte?" I asked.

"How did you see that link? Of course, they're buried close together." George looked about him and scratched his nose. "Got a picture of the Tower on the day it came down on top of poor Connie." He scrabbled among papers on his desk, "Ah, here we go", handing it to me; just a porch remaining, with a villager and two firemen standing at the door. "That's me", he said, pointing to one. "She stood no chance, of course, tons of stone on her. You see, she knew Mabel of old - perhaps knew her too well. They kept their distance. Lived at either end of the village. Mabel in her prefab, Connie in the Volta Tower with her father. Lived different lives too. Connie was one of those 'no good do gooders', was a staunch Christian, school mistress, always a kind word, couldn't fault the woman. Except perhaps too introverted, constantly fighting her shyness, her nerves, she was. Was alright with a class of children, but a bag of nerves with fellow adults."

"I suspected, and I wasn't alone, that the two deaths were connected. Connie conquered her worst fear, that of Mabel, her arch enemy, and confronted her at Mabel's doorstep. What with Mabel's caterwauling and Connie's quiet delivery, those witnessing the altercation only heard Mabel's half of the conversation. She was heard to say 'So what if I did!', 'Just you wait 'til she's released' (a reference to the doll, we took this as) and finally, decisively 'I'll bring her wrath down on you and anyone else as crosses me!'. Bring her wrath down on her, no less."

"So why didn't anyone do something when the tower came down?" I asked, incredulous.

"I'm ashamed to say we were afraid, those of us that murmured our suspicions. Afraid that the same would happen to us. And Mabel withdrew, became quiet again living alone, moved down to one of the charity cottages and was no more bother, so the suspicions faded, were replaced by an ever diminishing unease. As you've found too, how do you explain these things to the police? You'd be scoffed at, laughed out of the police station."

It was obvious that the unease was rekindled, the danger mounting.

"I don't want another death on my conscience", said George emotionally. "Not that I was to blame, but you know what I mean. I don't want my inaction to cause harm to someone else now. I'm afraid, I can't say I'm not. I'll help though, help however I can. We'll need God on our side as well and you say the vicar is with you?"

"Yes", I nodded, "the vicar's with me."

"That'll help", George said, as I got up to go.

I'd taken to sleeping on the vicar's couch those few nights, my wife and Emily sharing the spare room for safety sake and there being no other serviceable bedroom in the house. I took the week off work, as I felt I needed to be around. The night after I'd spoken to George, I had my worst 'nightmare' to date. It could have been explained away perhaps. Our conversation on the life of Mabel Hinde kept an air of foreboding hanging over me. Easy enough for ominous daytime preoccupations to turn into nocturnal visitations. Physical marks, signs of a struggle - perhaps indications of my tossing and turning. And some people do mark themselves without realising it or having any recollection after the fact.

However much I tried to rationalise my visions, I could not wholly rule out the possibility that it had actually happened.

I had settled down uncomfortably on the sofa, the embers of the fire emitting a faint red glow from the hearth. I remember growing tremendously hot and was sweating profusely. I sat up and looked at the mirror over the fire - it reflected the large Georgian window behind me. One that had been shuttered and curtained before I retired. Only now, the curtains and shutters were open and the sash was up. I turned swiftly to see the Dutch Doll crawling slowly towards me, like a large hunting cat. Its eyes were fixed on me and even when it noticed that it had been discovered, continued crawling and grinned broadly. The window blackened and I realised that another figure was climbing into the room. Mabel Hinde. She too walked over steadily, a wet oilskin cape draped over her and she was carrying a small hatchet in her right hand. Too half asleep and dumbstruck to move, I remained sitting bolt upright, unable to utter a word. The two creatures, for I regarded the old woman as no more human than the doll, came around to my side of the sofa. The doll lifted a wavering hand, then shot it out at my quilt, throwing it back to my knees. I could see Mabel trying to get into position with the hatchet now raised and in both hands. The Dutch Doll clawed hungrily at my ankles.

"There! There! He's mine now!" Mabel cried. This utterance roused me from my stupor and I leapt up, sending both figures that were over me tumbling in different directions. I roared with all my might (and this roar, at least, was real, for it woke the house) and dashed at them, striking the woman with my fist at her shoulder and kicking at the doll. I remember that hurting, as though I were kicking a piece of furniture. I delivered three or four kicks, which in themselves were propelling the doll in the direction of the window, before it managed to get to its feet and took a headlong dive into the shrubbery. I turned to face Mabel Hinde, but she had gone. Not a trace of her remained - she must have left by the window as I was attacking the doll, or left by another means.

Within thirty seconds, as I was refastening the windows and closing the shutters, Nick, Louise and Emily all piled into the room. I was glad to see that our girl was with them, as I didn't want her to be alone upstairs, or anywhere else, but I didn't want to alarm her. All I could say to the others at that stage was:

"From now on, Nick, I want you to lock all the doors and bolt all the windows - I think we've had visitors again tonight."

*"Some of old St Crispin's sons
Now labour there all day"*

VII

[1934: The decent of
Miss Mary Ozier]

Once the Dutch Doll had been taken into the church by the Reverend Samuel Paul, its malevolent influence appeared to diminish gradually. The Reverend never again saw any sign of movement, or hear any sound. He still felt a faint disquiet initially and proceeded to sprinkle holy water on the doll daily and say a short exorcising prayer. He noticed a very slight burning aroma when administering in this way to begin with, but this died down after a few weeks. Gradually, his practice of prayer fell away too, as did his fear. He could see the doll from his pulpit and even began to think light-heartedly of it after some years had passed; choosing to dismiss that night when he saw it move as a slight impression made upon him by the devil. His faith strengthened by the doll's subjugation, now it was in God's house. Despite his selective memory and the dulling of it, he fully intended to tell his successor the story, by way of an amusing anecdote. Unfortunately, he was not given the chance - he suffered a heart attack one day and was found in the churchyard by his wife, quite dead. He was still holding in his hand the spoon he used to stir his tea.

Mary Ozier's reaction to loosing the doll to the confines of the church could not have been more reactionary. The quiet sobbing she first exhibited gave way to uncontrolled wailing back at the school. Amy was left to look after the children and was forced to send the day girls away on the morning after the dramatic night and discovery of blood in the cellar. The police were conducting their rather ham-fisted forensics - methods that would never pass mustard these days - contaminating the evidence, stamping all over the 'crime scene' in their size nines, not to mention the omission of failing to analyse the doll. These comings and goings all punctuated a fraught day for Amy, who looked after the boarders well enough, but sooner or later had to face the fact that, with Miss Ozier incapable, she had to send the boarders away too - at least for the remainder of this term. By the end of the week, only two students remained. Mabel, who was provided for, but otherwise left unloved, by her only surviving relative, an elderly aunt. And Constance, whose mother was dead and father was overseas serving in the army. This left a very strange, almost abandoned house, with Amy perhaps the only occupant who was unaware of the pitching together of good and evil.

Mabel, as we might have expected by this stage in her tainting, spent more and more time with the inconsolable Miss Ozier. The headmistress was calmed somewhat by Mabel's presence at her bedside, which is more than can be said for the admittance of the doctor, who was sent from the house with a flea in his ear and an uncomfortable feeling that this woman ought to be committed. But he did no more about it. The vicar also called in that first week and, although encouraged by Amy, incited such howls from Miss Ozier upstairs, that he thought it best to retreat for a while.

The search for Hilda, the lost girl, continued. Not only the schoolhouse was searched, the surrounding houses, woodland, fields were scoured also, to no avail. Working men, friends of Hilda's parents and the local constabulary didn't shirk for three days. Slowly, the men were forced, resignedly, to return to their jobs on the farm, in the factories, the shops. The police too, scaled down their search, although kept a presence in the village. A sad acceptance that the girl was lost crept upon everyone. Only the girl's mother and father trudged on, circling the village, recounting their steps, time and time again.

In the schoolhouse, a cold war without borders formed. Neither side much molesting the other, just a brooding ambivalence. Amy took to sleeping in the dormitory with Constance, whilst Mary Ozier and Mabel stayed in Mary's room day and night, seldom stirring. Amy would occasionally enquire after Miss Ozier and when she did so, she would often find Mary and Mabel engaged in earnest conversation, whispering conspiratorially. They would take the cold fair that Amy brought to them and deposit the dirty dishes at the door. Otherwise, the pair would throw disdainful glances at Amy and little more. Amy purposely kept Constance away from the other two, taking her out on errands most days. She tried to keep the girl as cheerful as possible, playing games and distracting her with light schoolwork.

Constance, although trying not to be upset by recent events, could not stop herself from bringing her fears to the surface.

"I'm afraid, Miss, that Miss Ozier and Mabel will put me down in the cellar, like Mabel did with Hilda that time."

"Well, I'm with you", Amy reassured, "and I'll let nothing happen to you while I am. I've written to your father, *par avion,* they call it, by air, for his instructions on your care. If we get no reply within the month and if Miss Ozier hasn't come to her sen…. if she isn't better by then, then I'll take you to stay with me and my mother if need be. Though she's not in the best of health and I'll only to do that as a last resort." Secretly, Amy herself was very anxious in the present circumstance. Constance's insistence on recounting 'ghostly tales' didn't help.

"I think Miss Ozier and Mabel are in cahoots with the Dutch Doll and it was the doll that done for Hilda. Mabel looked so wild that night, I was petrified that she would set the doll on me. They've both given themselves over to the devil."

"Now less of that", Amy said, smoothing down Connie's hair, not wishing to hear any more, for fear of spooking herself further. "All I know is, Miss Ozier is not very well. Yes, I admit that the pair of them don't appear very kindly and we should have as little to do with them as possible. And soon, we'll leave them to it. Perhaps try and find Miss Ozier help and Mabel a place somewhere. But for now, we'll find our own safety first and think of them two later. Now, let's get ready for bed".

Amy brushed Connie's hair, her own black tresses brushed and tied back, and tried to settle down. The two on the floor below decided to set out from their self-imposed confinement. Miss Ozier was by now composed, though distant and hollow eyed and expressionless. Mabel kept the inane grin that she'd attained in the cellar on her encounter with the Dutch Doll and her learning of the secret incantation. They stood holding hands at Mary's bedroom door. Mary holding a carpet bag in one hand. Waiting for the last rays of natural light to slip away. As the final hint of sunshine left Mabel's eyes, she stared up at Mary Ozier, they tightened the grip of their joined hands and Mary slowly turned her door knob. Every move was deliberate and gentle, aware of creaky floorboards and hidden pieces of furniture. Taking the stairs gingerly, descending on toes and trying to rest weight out into the walls of the stairwell, there was the inevitable crack. At this, they would wince a little, stop, listen and begin again. Finally reaching the bottom, they turned mechanically into the passageway holding the cellar door. Both had but one aim; a plan of butchery, escape and flight. Rehearsed between them in the past few days, each had a part to play. But even the first necessity was forgotten in their excitement.

"The saw!" said Mary in delight and mock scolding directed at her little prodigy.

"Oh dear!" whispered Mabel, giggling to herself as she padded off to the kitchen. She returned in a moment with the little hacksaw that was kept for sawing through many a hard ingredient - coconut shell, crab claws, bones.

Carefully turning the cellar door lock and flicking on the light, the two figures could not contain their glee. Tripping down the first three steps, they paused at the familiar tiny inscription.

Mary held a finger to her pursed lips "Don't say it now - only when you need to, when it's time."

At the bottom, they admired their next beauty spot. Where blood spotted the flagstones. Falling to their knees in unison, hungry hands swept over the dried remnants of that sorry victim. They almost could have licked the brown patches, you would have thought, had you sight of the awful scene. Worse was to come.

Mary pulled herself up and gestured Mabel towards the large bookcase. It must have been built in the room - and hundreds of years old. "This'll be the most difficult part - every ounce of strength, we'll need - come on then." And with that Mary shifted her bulk against one end of the heavy oak piece. Mabel leant a hand too and, though is was hard to see how her slight efforts could have helped, together they edged the bookcase in a slow arc, in five stages. It needed to be two feet clear to give Mary access behind. With each move, there was a deep groan and with each groan they paused, took breath and looked skyward, as though they could see through three floors into the dormitory.

The movement of this colossal piece of furniture did resonate through the house and did vibrate as high up as the dormitory in which Amy and Constance were set-tling down. Though it was only nine o'clock, they were in bed, but not asleep. They looked at each other as the noises reverberated from below. It was like the distant sound of some hellish machine, there to inflict suffering with it's diabolical tone. These were not usual noises and with each abrasive shudder, Amy and Constance shuddered too.

"What on earth is that Miss?" uttered Constance in disbelief.

"Maybe something outside", said Amy at first, then, more worried, "or maybe something I need to check on." She stirred herself and gathered her dressing gown.

"Not without me!" panicked Constance, "you're not leaving me alone up here!"

"No. Alright then. But keep a safe distance behind me."

Back down in the cellar, Mary produced an oil lamp from the carpet bag and handed Mabel a small bundle of newspapers. "For wrapping", she said to Mabel with a tight smile. Lighting the oil lamp and holding it up behind the bookcase, Mary illuminated a neat little door, no more than four feet tall, of unfinished hard wood. It had a simple latch, with no lock or bolts. Lifting the latch and pushing the door open, Mary inhaled deeply as dank, cold, corrupted air rushed past her. She smiled back at Mabel and said: "Coming then? Are you ready?" Mabel nodded and smiled even broader, if that were possible. The headmistress ducked down through the door, followed by Mabel, who just needed to lower her head. And they were gone.

Meanwhile, Amy and Constance had reached the ground floor. They were as quiet as can be and realised, to their horror, that the cellar door was open. Amy ushered the girl out into the entrance hall, silently undid the front door and whispered into Connie's ear "you wait here, stand in the doorway for one half minute, while I get a policeman. They're all over the village - there's bound to be one within a few yards."

Constance stood hesitantly at the door, her head darting inside, then out.

In the school cellar end of the tunnel, Mary and young Mabel did not have far to go to find what they

went there for. Something that half the village had
been looking for for the last five days - the crumpled
body of Hilda Dixon. She lay apparently awake,
frozen in wide-eyed petrifaction. The poor girl's former teacher and protector dropped down to the body
eagerly. She beckoned Mabel to bring over the carpet
bag. From it she quickly extracted a pair of needlework scissors and the kitchen saw. She sized up the ankles, already lightly shredded by the attentions of her
murderer. Lifting one leg up, she studied the Achilles
tendon, before snipping into it decisively with the sharp
scissors. Because Hilda had been dead for days, there
was no rush of blood. Clear liquid oozed from the in-
cision. Next Mary signalled for the small silver hacksaw. As she gripped the girl's shin and began sawing,
she nodded to Mabel, saying:

"I think it's time to use it now, in the hopes that it
will bring greater power, some life, to this act." They
began the majik rhyme that Mabel had learnt a week or
so before, the one that had taken her over so, the one
that, fifty years later, I had heard in a dream, but was
afraid to recount:

"Hell is the cauldron and the devil is the spoon."
Over and over again they repeated this horrible mantra,
rising in pitch and volume, as Mary carried out her griz-
zly business. She was through and had severed one foot
and had placed it on a sheet of newspaper and was starting on the other, when a sound made them both stop in
their tracks. Someone was coming!

The pair dropped their tools and rushed out back into
the cellar, before a startled Constance could collect
herself. Constance had heard the compelling rhyme
being chanted and it had somehow drawn her down into

the cellar. Unnaturally and against her deepest fears, she found herself standing on the cellar flags, suddenly faced with this unholy pair. Animal-like, Mary and Mabel quickly encircled Constance. Assessing the situation, Mary eyed Connie up and down, especially down.

"Yes, that will be much better!" Mary rasped as she and Mabel descended upon Constance. They took her by one arm each and pulled her viciously back into the tunnel.

Amy was wide-eyed with horror at the sight of the empty doorway as she returned with PC Harry Bankes and two of his fellow constables. She scouted frantically around the hallway and used a restrained whispering call to flush out Constance from the schoolroom, without success. A stifled scream permeated from the passageway at the back. The policemen lost no time in marching to the head of the cellar stairs. Great lumbering steps they took as they disappeared noisily into the basement. Amy followed quickly behind, her heart pounding in sheer terror, her mind racing ahead to unimaginable scenes of blood and violence. For a second, the three men blundered seemingly blind around the cellar, until one noticed the shifted bookcase and dim light emanating from behind it.

"Harry, behind this!" the constable yelled. PC Bankes immediately got his bulk around the solid oak and threw his weight into a sudden heave that moved the bookcase another foot into the room and allowed him access into the tunnel. The entrance darkened as he occupied it and two seconds later he could be heard shouting "hey there! Leave her alone!" The two other policemen followed Harry Bankes into the tunnel and Amy crouched at the doorway.

What Harry saw both deeply shocked him and spurred him into action. Mary and Mabel were bent over two little girls. One still, grey and...cut up...the other trying to cry out through a hand on her mouth and thrashing as much as she could with three more hands holding her. One of Connie's ankles was bloody. Harry launched himself at Mary Ozier, knocking Mabel down and the headmistress away down the tunnel.

"Come ere!" Harry bellowed as he stumbled after Mary, who had grabbed at her oil lamp as she passed it. The other officers took a struggling Mabel and a panting Constance back out into the cellar to Amy.

Mary charged down the tunnel towards its crossroads as fast as she could manage. She'd gained a good five yards when she reached a prop that split the passageway in two. Seeing her opportunity and wishing to grasp it, Mary took hold of the prop and gave it a quick yank, pulling back with her full weight whilst hanging onto it. She had hoped to dislodge a brick or two and slow Harry Bankes down. She under-estimated the extent to which the tunnel's structure relied on that support. The timber came crashing down under a cloud of dust and dirt, followed without delay by a half-ton of bricks, rubble and earth. Harry skidded to a halt and fell back with inches to spare. Mary was buried to her chest and let out a desperate groan.

Hearing this back in the cellar, Mabel struggled free of her captor and rushed headlong back into the tunnel.

"Let me see her!" Mabel yelled as she reached her crushed companion.

"This is no place for you young girl - if this lot collapses again, we'll be for it." said PC Bankes, thinking of his own neck as much as Mabel's

"Here, here!" Mary let out, putting out her one free arm to the girl.

"I can't be held responsible, no one could say I haven't done my bit", said Harry Bankes as he retreated slowing back to the tunnel entrance. In the dim, dust-filled passage, Mary and Mabel exchanged their last few words, as Mary slipped away.

"There's no use Mabel, I can feel that I'm beyond help", began Mary. "But you must do something for me." Mabel leant over her old school ma'am, giving absolute undivided attention, without a care for her own safety, but every care to saviour the last instructions of her mistress.

Gasping more and more between each word, Mary continued: "Don't forget what I've taught you. You know how to conjure up. You know how to act as mistress yourself. Secure, when you can, the Dutch Doll's release. Its like a prison for her in there, but she's still with us, we can still feel her, can't we?"

"Yes Mary", the young girl replied, using Miss Ozier's first name for the first time, with increasing confidence, increasing knowledge of her own destiny. "I'll keep a watch and I'll be here when she's free again. And I'll make sure she gets what she wants."

With this, Mary appeared momentarily at ease, until a sudden dreadful pain shot through her from embedded limbs and torso. "There's my darling, there's my dear girl", she managed to say at last, reaching up to feel Mabel's hair, before finally rasping out her last breath. A black shadow formed over her, so it seemed to Mabel. Mary's gentle caress turned instantly to a desperate death reflex grab at Mabel's tresses. Mabel was pulled ferociously to the ground and she felt a sudden rush of air downwards, as though a tree had been felled right by her, had missed her by a hair's breadth. Then the air cleared, Mary's grip fell away and the noise of those back in the cellar returned to Mabel's hearing.

The next day, the tunnels were opened up fully by the police. In broad daylight their expanse became known and fully mapped out. Hilda's body was removed and a post mortem conducted. The cause of death was found to be strangulation. Mabel was questioned at the local police station. To all the questions: "What did you see of Miss Ozier in the cellar?", "Did you know Hilda was trapped down there?" , "Did you see her killed?", to all these and more, Mabel remained silent. The police had Connie's story, that implicated Mabel, but this was one girl's word against another. And Mabel was clever enough to realise this and keep quiet.

Miss Ozier was dug out and given a hasty cremation. Amy testified to her old employer's cruelty to her charges and candid about her reasons for doing nothing. She was afraid for herself and for the girls. She never expected anything as serious as this to happen.

The police had their suspect, with damning character witnesses aplenty, conveniently dead. Even if she had survived, Mary Ozier would have been content to have 'taken the rap', understanding that it was time, in the present circumstances, to protect the knowledge of the Dutch Doll, pass on the knowledge and protection to someone younger who might be more able to make use of it. Officially, the doll was never implicated and how could it be, without individuals risking their own standing in the village, risking public humiliation at being branded a fantasist.

As I have said, the doll's apparent influence faded with the vicar's daily prayer. What was unseen and unfelt was the still beating heart. Not a literal heart, with pumping cavities and valves; an impenetrable living core, withdrawn from the outside world, forced by it's severe environs to sit and wait.

And wait it did, for forty seven years. It's protector still living, waiting also.

Some folks have taken on themselves,
To alter all its laws

VIII

[1981 - A confrontation]

It was with mixed emotions that I brought my family back into the old schoolhouse. On the one hand, relieved that the repair work was completed with little fuss, the fire damage rectified, everything as good as new. On the other, a certain dread that our haunting would follow us back. The 'occurrences' appeared to afflict us wherever we were - we seemed to be equally at peril in the vicarage as at home. We did seriously consider moving away, perhaps having a holiday to see if that would rid us of our demons. But my work beckoned again and, besides, why should we be frightened away? So a firm decision to return home was made. Made bravely and resolutely in a daylight hour. Fears returned all too easily come nightfall and when Emily had been safely tucked in, Nick paid us a reassuring visit and one with a practical purpose.

"I would like, if I may, to conduct an exorcism", he pronounced matter-of-factly. "We don't get much call for them these days, but I think, in the present climate, a few prayers, a blessing, a sprinkling of holy water, could bring you the peace of mind..." he hesitated, "...the protection that you need."

Louise and I acquiesced without resistance. My experience on the vicar's couch had convinced me of an evil presence at large in the old part of the village, one that we needed protection from. So Nick proceeded through the house, repeating the same prayer in each room:

"Our Lord Saviour protect all in this house from the evil one and all his accomplices; bring this family peace and safety through Your loving presence. Amen." Then splashing a few drops of bless-laden water before moving on. He even whispered the same words, perhaps more earnestly, inside Emily's bedroom door. When he'd finished, we came and sat awhile at the hearth.

"I do hope that comforts you. And I wonder whether tomorrow I should start to do more. To seek out this wickedness amongst us and try to drive it out. First, I need to speak to my bishop, or at least my own priest, for guidance. It would be foolish to do anything alone."

"If this...thing and Mabel Hinde are intent on causing us harm, if they do want something of us [at that moment I knew not what; suspected a terrifying fascination with feet, but could not speak my fears out loud] then I think its only right that we should go on the attack - come out fighting. And you're right to seek help Nick - you and 'your lot' are better equipped than I am to handle this."

We parted happily, though part of us wanted to hang on and keep Nick with us longer. As it happened, that first night back in the house passed uneventfully. Maybe the blessings and protection from the church had helped. I spent a restless night, listening out for any sound, one eye open for any shift of door or curtain.

Only at dawn did I feel relaxed enough to catch a couple of hours of sleep.

I spent the day at work wistfully, distracted, preoccupied. Happy at least that we'd all been left in peace. When I returned home I found that the night had not gone entirely uneventfully. Louise was waiting at the roadside when I pulled up.

"Nick's been taken ill", she opened without preamble. "He's quite bad, apparently. I heard the news at the corner shop. Nothing specific, just that he was in hospital."

"Hospital? No", I rejected, as one does when faced with bad news. Then I thought for a second. "Maybe we should go over to the vicarage to see if anyone's there... if anyone has news."

We followed a column of smoke back to its source and found old Fred, the vicar's gardener, burning leaves in a steel bin. He told us what he knew.

"I came up early, as usual, to see if the vicar wanted me to fetch anything from the shops in town, before I started work. Now, he'd be up normally, over at the church for eight, ready for matins. But no sign of him and no answer at the door. The regular half-dozen by the church door, starting to get restless. Mrs Dunkley came over and we discussed what to do. In the end I got my spare key hidden in the potting shed and we opened up. Still no answer and no sign about the ground floor, so Mrs D and me went up to his room. There he was. Bedclothes in disarray, curtains thrown back and the vicar slumped at the window. Good job we arrived when we did. He was moaning very slightly, but we couldn't rouse him. Semi-conscious, I'd say. Then he drifted off. We called the ambulance. I telephoned a half hour ago.

His ward sister says he's not in danger, but still not awake. They found an irregular heart beat, she said; wonder if it might be a heart attack or stroke."

"No sign...of a break in, or anything?" I asked.

"No", George replied.

As we walked back to the house, I wondered if Nick had seen something, whether the Dutch Doll or Mabel Hinde had tried to get at him. "I think he got some of the poison that I had forced on me the other night. He may have had a visit." Louise knew what I meant and suggested we go over to the hospital. "Not this evening", I suggested, "not if he's not regained consciousness. You take Emily and go over to your mother's. I'm going to speak to George Mason again. He's on our side. He understands the threat that faces us. Perhaps he'll have an idea."

"OK, but be careful and come and let us stay in a hotel tonight. I don't feel at all comfortable about the house as things stand."

"Alright, I agree - I'll give you a call later."

I saw my wife and daughter off and walked over to George's. It was dusk and a mist was descending. Curling 'round the houses like cotton-gloved fingers. George was just coming out of his flat door as I was about to knock on it. He was on his way to the Bell Inn, his local.

"Come and join me", he offered, when I asked him for ten minutes of his time. On the way over, back along Church Street, around by my house and up the Bell Hill, I related news of the vicar's illness. George had heard, but not the detail that I was able to give him - and of course we could both share the special significance that only Dutch Doll aficionados could read into the news.

"So you think that Mabel and the doll somehow got to the vicar and almost...scared him to death?" George asked, or else shared my conclusion.

"Exactly", I affirmed, pushing open the door of the pub. "Nick was quite open minded about the existence of an 'evil force' behind the doll; said that it was part of his calling - his faith - if you like, to acknowledge the existence of the devil and his many and various fork-carriers."

We eyed each other knowingly, as if to say, without the need to speak the words: 'hush now, wait until the coast is clear, until we're not overheard, before resuming our highly sensitive and incredulous conversation'. Resume it, we did, after buying a couple of pints and depositing them on the small table next to George's favourite chair by the fire.

"All this totally convinces me that the Dutch Doll exerts such a power, born of some satanic catalyst in the distant past and will go on wielding this power, hurting, even killing, at least turning them away from the 'right path' for a very long time. Possibly for ever, if some-thing's not done..." Here George tailed off, for he knew that something must be done and that he was afraid to face it. But rather aptly, Dutch courage began to embrace us with the nerve. To dare to act.

"I think we need to call on widow Hinde", I blurted out bravely, testing the waters. George was very worried, but didn't wish to look a coward. With not altogether mock apprehension, he said:

"I'm right behind you."

We set off back down the hill. It was very cold, but the low cloud and mist was keeping the frost at bay. We could barely see twenty yards ahead; buildings loomed up one by one. Tingdene Cottage, the schoolhouse and it's neighbours and, as we walked up the alleyway leading to the rear, the small neat row of almshouses. Mabel's was the one second from the end. The others were all occupied by single pensioners or elderly couples. They each had a simple layout; a single storey with small porch and sitting room at the front, kitchen, the only bedroom and bathroom at the back. Open on a narrow path at each front door, with enclosed low-walled rear gardens. There were occasional lights, signs of habitation, except for Mabel Hinde's, which was shrouded in darkness, unkempt and dirty looking. No evidence of care or attention. George and I paused at the door of black studded oak. I took the knocker in trembling hand, held it there for a long second, then rapped forcibly four times. Not a sound. I knocked again. Still nothing. Finally, feeling emboldened by the thought of a harmless empty house, I pushed the letterbox open to see what I could see. Something hard met my fingers - met mine, rather than me meeting it, I thought. I recoiled and retreated a step or two.

"There's someone, something, in there!" I whispered to George.

"And there's two of us out here", George replied. "Whatever it is, if we approach it together, we'll be safer than we would be alone. I'm for going on. Come on!" he said, suddenly seized by an urge to lay an old burden to rest. He seized the door knocker once more, rapped sharply at it and shouted, "Come on now Mabel, we know you're in there. Come and show yourself to George Mason." A neighbouring old gentleman quivered at his net curtains for a moment, saw that something was about to start that he didn't want to get involved with and withdrew as quick as he appeared. George continued quieter at Mabel Hinde's door, "You remember old George. We're not here to do you any harm, we just want to talk something over, try to come to some sort of agreement, resolution if you like, to that matter we're both familiar with." There was a shuffling sound from inside, then the sound of the door chain being attached, then the door came open three inches. Mabel's face appeared in the chink, furrowed forehead, unkempt hair, blazing eyes.

"What on earth are you two after, at this time!" Mabel spat out as she eyed us up.

"Come now, Mabel", said George, more resolute than ever, "this is no time at all to you. You're a night owl alright. Rarely seen out in daylight! We just want to talk to you about the happenings of the last few days."

"What 'happenings'?" she shot back, "Nothing to do with me, his girl or the vicar."

"On the defensive again?" I ventured. "You were a bit more forthcoming the other morning. You know what I saw. I saw you and that...creature. There's a leash between you, I know that much. Which of you wears it about the neck, and which one tugs at the other end, I'm unsure, but you and it are tied together and act together. And you two are responsible for the abduction of my girl and the illness inflicted on the vicar."

"And what do you hope to gain by knocking on my door?" Mabel sneered back. George and I looked at each other. We didn't actually have a plan of action or any aim, besides 'disarming' Mabel and the doll.

"We mean to stop you!" said George half defiant, with enough uncertainty to make Mabel realise that she perhaps had the upper hand still.

"What I do and yes, what my friend does too", Mabel said with a knowing smile, "is well beyond your control. We can't be stopped. Do you mean to murder me, a poor old woman? Or go to the police with a cock-and-bull story about wooden spectres?"

"Whatever it takes, we'll do", continued George. "As we're all now under no illusions and I've told this young man as much as I know about the events of '34, we will stop you. Because we know that the alternative is to leave the two of you free to roam and that could lead to...could lead to..."

"To more death, more harm done", I finished for George. "The two thieves dead in the last few weeks, and what I'd call two further attempted murders since. At least one death that we know about in the thirties; your husband; that woman in the Volta Tower. And God knows what's happened outside our knowledge. You're right, we don't have many options, but we are determined. You'll not carry on like this. We'll not let you!"

"I'm not listening to anymore of this rubbish", said Mabel, "You do your worst and see what becomes of you!" She tried to shut her door, but I stuck my foot in it. "Get out of it!" Mabel screamed and banged the door against my foot twice more. I held fast. Mabel suddenly disappeared from view and we could hear sounds of movement retreating into the cottage.

"We've got to carry on as we've started", George said at my side. I nodded agreement and put my shoulder to the door. And again. And once more before the chain gave way and I found myself tumbling into Mabel's porch. It was pitch dark, it at first seemed - although becoming accustomed, I could see a human form over me that I soon realised was a coat stand, dressed in ragged black. There was a musty aroma, a dampness that filled my nostrils. I raised myself up quickly as George stepped over the threshold and felt around for a light. By the door, 'click, click, click', no light. We both looked up to the empty bulb socket above our heads.

"Should've come prepared, with a torch or something", said George, then louder into the house: "Come on Mabel, let's have no more messing about, we mean business and we mean to stop you. It'll save you a lot of grief (and me, George thought), if you listen to us. We're not going away. Come and talk - we can help you if you're trapped in some way."

More scuffling and then something that sounded like crockery breaking, then a shout from the far interior: "You leave me alone! I don't need help. You'll be for it. I'll call the police - or worse!" she ended.

"She's getting out the back, come on" I said to George and we made our way through the gloomy woollen sitting room into the kitchen. The back door had just slammed shut and something was being wedged behind it. "She's put a chair or something against it on the outside", I snarled in frustration, as I rattled the door. We tried the kitchen window; not opened in many years by the feel of it and unlikely to open now, before finding the bedroom at the back. It had a large dark wardrobe and dressing table with mirror at the window. The curtains at it fell away from their pole in a haphazard way and the bedclothes were similarly dishevelled and crumpled in a mass. We went to the window and struggled with that too, again to no avail.

"Look!" said George, pointing out through the dirty pane at the figure of Mabel Hinde, springing with surprising agility over her back wall. And not just that. The dome of a head bobbing along beside her as she darted away to our left. We knew very well what this head was and the head itself instantly recognised that it had eyes upon it. Two small dark hands curled over the top of the wall. A bonneted head raised itself up, as if to look at us. We could see no facial features, except for the faint trace of a line of a nose.

"Well, I'll be blowed! There she is!" was all George could utter before the doll dropped back down and joined its' companion. "We'll have to get after them", George put to me.

"Without a light - it would be impossible on a night like this", I suggested. "Much better to make use of our criminal break in and have a look around." George conceded with a grunt. We first looked around Mabel's bedroom. Turning on the bare electric light, we surveyed the scene. As I've said, a pile of bedclothes on the double bed. Unmade and unclean. A peek inside the wardrobe revealed just a few Spartan items; grey or back dresses and skirts. The bottom was filled with newspapers, some very old - and a scrapbook with a pair of scissors. Unearthing it, we thumbed a few pages. Clippings from the 1930's about the disappearance and death of Hilda Dixon. The collapse of the Volta Tower. And lastly loose scraps detailing the recent news of the church robbery, the car crash, the Dutch Doll missing.

"Just like all the best psychopaths", I commented wryly to George, "she likes to keep a record of her achievements." We looked in each of the drawers of the dressing table. They contained a strange miscellany of potting shed bric-a-brac. Lengths of twine, small jars of turpentine and...and an old packet of rat poison.

"What did for her husband, no doubt", concluded George darkly.

Switching off the bedroom light, we moved back into the kitchen, flicking on the intermittent semaphore of the florescent tube. Most immediately apparent were the small glass bottles on the table, half a dozen of them, most with stoppers, a couple without. George sniffed at one.

"Phew!...urine!" he exclaimed.

"Her own do you think? How peculiar."

"Not as strange as you'd think", George explained. "You see, those that conduct spells, witches if you want too call them that, often use their own urine as a powerful ingredient."

Something suddenly clicked. "So that's what I saw when I went to see her husband's grave - she was pissing on it." I was somewhat taken aback by the suggestion. George contemplated:

"It may be - and this is just an educated guess, I don't know much about witchcraft - it may be that the ingredient is made more potent if generated in a particular location. Makes it full of voodoo."

We further investigated the contents of the kitchen. Little food - raw beef in the refrigerator, some canned vegetables and fruit. And, more frighteningly, a vast array of kitchen implements, of the cutting variety. Knives, cleavers, saws and spikes, amassed on the draining board as if making ready for war. Perhaps she was, I thought.

"This woman and her...accomplice...are even more dangerous than we imagined George", I said. I was going to say 'we'll need reinforcements before tackling them', but was cut short by a scuffing at the front door.

I switched the light off, plunging us into darkness. "She's come back George - be careful", I whispered intently. A torch beam scoured the sitting room ahead of us. Not her - I suddenly felt relieved.

"Who's that back there? Now don't try anything. This is the police." Never before had I been so glad to be arrested.

In the police car returning to the station, I wondered whether we should have concocted some story about being neighbours (which I was) and discovering a break-in. But we were caught red handed, in a dark house with the door kicked in. If the truth be told, we were glad to be away and safe. Louise and Emily were away for the night too, Nick was in hospital and George and I were facing at least a night in the cells. Short-term, I thought, none of us could come to the sort of harm that we were most afraid of.

"I wonder if anyone else is on their 'hit list'?" I asked out loud.

"Be quiet", said the officer in front.

Nor let the ghost at present fly,
Nor let the noises budge

IX

[1981, continued]

Separated and questioned into the early hours, George and I (we later conferred) kept our stories safely away from the paranormal, rather to the facts. At my interview was Inspector Richard Vines, the policeman who was in charge of the search for Emily. His suspicion had been aroused at the sound of my name in the charge room. I'd waived my right to a solicitor and sat alone with him in the stark little cell of an interview room.

"Your daughter is alright now?" he began, head down looking at the charge sheet. He was tired, I could tell, at the end of a long shift, no doubt. His face was grey, his furrowed forehead pained and his eyes dark rimmed.

"Yes, pretty well recovered, although she had quite a traumatic experience. She and my wife are staying away tonight for a break from...it all."

"So you and your friend decided to take advantage of your free night and do a bit of house breaking, eh?", Vines came straight out with it. Not a vicious accusation, just delivered with worn out sarcasm.

"George and I had reason to believe that Mrs Hinde was up to something, needed to confront her and after an argument with her at the door, I'll admit, I barged my way in. I'll accept full responsibility for that. But we felt that Mrs Hinde was planning to commit more serious crimes."

"Murder, I suppose, this seventy year old woman?"

"Not quite as old as she looks", I answered.

"Still, not much of a danger to the community", stated Vines, fiddling with his pencil. "I had a chat with her, on the morning your daughter turned up. She was out walking early that morning, said she didn't sleep well and was usually up and out before dawn. Made a note of her name."

"Yes, I saw her too that morning", I said, "Just before I came back to find that Emily had returned."

"And you link the two events do you? You didn't care to mention this to me that day? You know we take a very dim view of people taking the law into their own hands."

"I'm sorry, but..." and here I paused to find the right tack, so as not to make the story sound too fantastical, "...but yes, I did suspect Mrs Hinde of being somehow involved in my daughter's disappearance. When I met her on the road she was not at all sympathetic and it was not so much what she said, but her manner - quite cynical - that made me think she might have abducted Emily."

"But all your daughter would talk about was the Dutch Doll", said Vines. I tried not to look startled at the mention of the name. Luckily Vines was scribbling. "Got it into her head after that break-in at the church and those two men dying." He and I exchanged weak smiles as an acknowledgement of the wild fairy tail. He continued: "she didn't mention Mrs Hinde or anyone else."

"No", I said, "I just drew an uncomfortable feeling from my meeting with Mrs Hinde on the road - nothing I could come to the police about - and felt that I needed to ask her a few questions. And as I've said, I'm admitting that I did shoulder the door open. Your officers did see what we saw in her kitchen. Stacks of knives and saws."

"Knives in a kitchen?", Vines laughed, "Whatever next!" Then after thinking for a second, "Wc will pay Mrs Hinde a visit, of course, if only because she's been a victim of crime. You'd better call a lawyer in the morning. You'll be appearing before the magistrates at 10.15. My guess is you'll need bail to see daylight. In the meantime you can consider your actions in the cells." And with a screech of his wooden chair on the tile floor, he was gone and I was being led away.

After an uncomfortable, though mercifully dream-free night, George and I went through an automatic court process. We were both bailed to appear in one month to face breaking and entering charges. We were out by noon and I phoned in work sick - something I'd never done before, but I needed thinking time, needed to work out how to break the news of my new criminal career. I used the opportunity to visit Nick in hospital. He was not as bad as we first thought. He was being kept in for a day or two for tests; the doctors still suspected a heart scare of some kind. He looked drawn, much more gaunt, frail even, than when we last met. But he managed to raise a weak smile or two. When we'd finished with the hospital visitor's niceties, bunch of grapes on the bedside cabinet, Nick started to retell of his brush with the Dutch Doll.

"I'd retired fairly soon after I returned from the exorcism at your house", he began in low tones, as an ominous wind whipped up outside to give the appropriate accompaniment. "Very soon after I'd gone to bed - I was still in the half way house between consciousness and sleep - I heard a tapping at my window. Not exactly a tapping, but a sound I took to be the sound of gravel being thrown from the driveway below. To attract my attention. I thought it was you, though I was puzzled as to why you hadn't just rung the door bell. Perhaps you had rung and it hadn't roused me sufficiently - that was my natural reasoning. When I opened my curtains, I could see nothing below, no one on the lawn or drive. I became more wary, but opened the window an inch or two. No sound. Then suddenly another spray of gravel, one or two chips stinging my face as they came in the house. I shouted then, 'who's there?' I naturally asked. I was more curious than worried at this stage. Again, not a sound. The next thing I did was the foolish move, the one all the stupidest characters in books and films succumb to. The need to go down and investigate. But you understand that although I was aware of what could be down there, I assumed that I had an 'earthly' visitor for some reason. Maybe I'd been fortified myself by the exorcism; thought I was invincible."

Nick smiled another weak smile, took a sip of water and continued: "I donned my overcoat, took my torch and opened the front door. There was absolutely nothing in my line of vision. I called 'hello' and, again, no response. So I stepped out. My second and last foolish mistake. They leapt upon me as soon as I was clear of the house. I couldn't believe it. I know you'd told me about her 'other side', as it were, but I just couldn't comprehend how this woman, rather cantankerous but otherwise normal woman, had turned into this wild-eyed banshee and had actually felled me in my own garden!" He paused, obviously still aghast at the idea.

"You say 'they' leapt upon you. So you saw the doll too?" I asked.

"Not at first, merely felt a third hand tugging at my collar. Then I fell onto my back. Hinde was sitting on my chest and I looked back and could see the Dutch Doll. And this was the worst part. It was laughing at me. 'Don't you struggle priest", Hinde was saying. I could hardly breathe, let alone move. The doll was dancing around, as if in victory. 'You'll not be the first priest that the Dutch Doll has taken, eh my friend?' the woman said. Then, to add to my shock, the doll spoke. 'I like priests', she said, in a girl's voice, ice cold and gleeful. This finally galvanised me. I threw up my chest and this unsteadied the old woman. She let go of one of my hands and I managed some how to tug her off me. As she was sprawling away, I lifted myself and pelted headlong for the door. They were right at my heels, I could feel, but I didn't look back. As I slammed the door shut behind me, I felt two thuds at it from the other side. I raced up to my room, with an infernal racket going on below. My heart was going like the clappers and I passed out at the foot of my bed. Next thing I knew it was light and old Fred and Mrs Dunkley were trying to rouse me. The thing that I couldn't fathom out is why that animalistic pair did not pursue me into the house."

"It sounds like they couldn't come in, otherwise why entice you outside in the first place?" I theorised. "They could both get into the vicarage when they attacked me, so its not the building itself that repels them."

"Evidence, as if I needed it, of the power of prayer", Nick became enlightened. "Before I went to bed, I anointed the vicarage, said a little prayer in each of the rooms, as I had done at yours. Well, a perfect piece of good supernaturalism." Nick smiled, a broader, less wearisome smile, as he concluded to himself, "At least one weapon we have in our armoury, one that we know works."

"Yes", I replied, less sceptical than I would have been a couple of weeks before. I related to Nick the 'adventure' that George and I played in the night before. Nick was very concerned:

"If, as I suspect, neither you nor George are possessed of the Holy Spirit - that is the sad fact, is it? That you have not embraced Jesus Christ in your lives?" I shook a sorrowful head. "If that's the case, then you are not able to use the one thing that we can say for certain can disable, or at least hinder, the Dutch Doll. I'm no expert in demonology and I can only guess at the relationship between Mrs Hinde and the doll. There is no doubt, however, that she is in the hands of the devil. She too, can only be saved, I hope saved rather than destroyed, by a greater force for good. You and George could learn and incant a prayer or two, but I doubt that without real faith behind them, they're likely to protect you. My advice is to stay well clear until I get out. I'll be released tomorrow, I'm sure. If I'm not, I'll discharge myself. I'd do it today, only, I've hardly took a step and I'm not sure…"

"Of course you should stay in today. At the very least. And don't worry about George and me. We'll be careful. And no more nocturnal escapades without you", I reassured.

Inspector Vines was good to his word and did call on Mabel Hinde that same afternoon. He knocked on the damaged front door several times before Mabel appeared at the sitting room window, obviously just woken from her beauty sleep.

"Who on earth's this, I was *trying* to rest", she admonished. Then, seeing Vines and a uniformed WPC, her face brightened into a ghoulish feigned delight. "Oh, it's you Inspector and...cr?"

"I have WPC Griffiths with me Mrs Hinde. Is it alright if we come in?"

"Of... of course Inspector", Mabel replied falteringly. "But you'll need to come around the back. Those vandals put paid to my door working, I'm afraid. I expect that's what you're here about? Well, I won't settle for anything less than full compensation, I feel defiled, I do..." and she faded into the house. Vines and Griffiths picked their way around to the kitchen door.

"...They were intent on getting in, at whatever cost", Mabel continued unabated opening the kitchen door. There was no sign of the bottles that George and I had seen the night before and no sign of the exotic cutlery either.

"I've spoken to them both and both admit to breaking and entering. They've been bound over to appear before the magistrate again in thirty days", Vines commented distractedly as he surveyed the kitchen.

"Released? I'm absolutely disgusted!" expelled Mabel.

"Yes, that's what I'd expect in a case such as this. And most likely you will be awarded compensation and costs, so no need to worry on that score. But I would like to know what caused the altercation at your door last night." Mabel winced slightly at Vines' line of questioning. She bought some time by ushering her guests into her sitting room. She drew the dusty curtains back fully and a cascade of particles, picked out by the low bright sunlight, swirled about the room. There was a shabby corduroy sofa and chair, a dark wood sideboard with radio atop, Gauguin's picture of the green faced woman on the wall and very little else. Mabel offered them tea while they took stock of this bare room. Presently, Mabel returned with two cups and muddy brown liquid, nothing for herself. Griffiths took one look at the tea and eyed Vines disdainfully. But after a pause, they both sipped out of politeness.

"As I was asking, Mrs Hinde", Vines finally resumed, "what was the argument about that preceded the breaking down of your front door?"

"Well, the two of them arrived here, it must have been after ten o'clock, obviously drunk, 'cos I could smell the beer on 'em", her defence began. "The two of 'em started off calling me all sorts of names and making nonsense accusations. I told 'em to go away and come back when they were both sober."

"And what were these accusations about?" asked Vines, knowing very well, but becoming strangely disinterested.

"Nonsense about that girl of his, as you know very well", soothed Mabel, glancing over to Griffiths and nodding a smile to her.

"Yes, that nonsense", repeated Vines. "And er…" he said, shaking his head, as though to shake off approaching sleep, "where did you then go to, having been forced from you're house? You didn't return until next morning, my officers said. They had to secure and stay by your cottage all night."

"Stayed with a friend of mine", said Mabel without a glimmer. The Inspector and his Constable continued to sip away, increasingly oblivious to it's sourness and the clouding of their judgement. No, more than clouding; something that turned it on it's head.

As Vines and Griffiths were shown out, Vines was sure that there was more that he wanted to ask, a vague feeling that there was something missing. At the same time, however, an inner voice was telling him, 'everything is in order; there's nothing else for you here'. Eerily, although again Vines only felt an ounce of this unease, Griffiths confirmed:

"Nothing else for us here".

Mabel was pouring the remains of the tea into her sink with a chuckle. She glanced at the tealeaf pattern on the bottom of Vines' cup before declaring in artificial prophesy: "A bright future for you my boy, but you'll not be coming here again." She turned back into her bedroom and swung open the wardrobe door to reveal the Dutch Doll, propped up in the corner, its stumps embedded in the pile of papers at the bottom. Mabel stroked its face, with all the affection that a mother would her child, only with awe and wonder too. The doll's right eye glistened as Mabel hummed, almost purred with delight.

Early that evening, I visited George to recount my conversation with the vicar and warn him against going out after dark. I passed on Nick's warning to us amateurs to stay clear of trouble.

"I won't take too much persuading to stay in tonight", said George, switching on his table lamp, dumping the evening paper on the floor amongst the rest and offering me a seat.

"No thanks George, I've got to get back to Louise and Emily; I just popped back to pick up a change of clothes. I'll feel more confident when the vicar's back in town and we have God on our side. Maybe we'll come back to stay in the schoolhouse tomorrow night if he's been discharged."

"Alright then. Oh, I've just come across a poem from an old village book that you'd be interested in"

"A poem?", I asked bemused.

"Yes, an ode to the village ghost written one hundred and fifty years ago. I'll let you borrow it...tomorrow, perhaps. I just have some reading to finish off before I do", George said, patting a faded brown leather volume, open and face down on the arm of his chair.

"Take care then; see you tomorrow"

"Don't worry about me", finished George, "I'll look after myself, keep the door and windows locked, not stir for anyone until the cock crows. I'm looking forward to a quiet night in with my book." And with that he waved me off into the dusky evening.

I walked back along to my house and gathered together another day's change of clothes. As I was packing them into the car, I had a terrible urge to go back in, to check out the cellar again. I watched the sun dipping below the horizon in a blaze of orange and yellow, in horror despite its beauty. I was beginning to develop a Van-Helsing-like dread of the night. With the dark came uncertainty, a creeping death to plague us all, a real danger that seeped into every pore. The horror was only matched by my nagging curiosity and while a patch of sunlit sky remained, I felt relatively safe.

I descended the stairs two at a time and stood at the bottom, breathing heavily. It was a degree or two colder than outside, but that I would have expected. Every sense became sharper. I could smell the coal, the damp wood. I could hear every sound; the birds in the distance outside over the beat of my own heart. And I could feel every fluctuation of air. It felt like breathing. At first, I thought it was my own breathing, then I realised that it was detached from me and slower than my own pace. A drawing in from behind, very slightly caressing my neck, circling my ears. Then an exhalation at my front, warmer in my face, with a odour of ashes. Very quickly, I felt myself becoming intoxicated with it, could feel myself swaying in tune with this other-worldly breathing. The cellar walls *looked* like they were expanding and contracting, developing a organic life of their own. I felt as if I was going to fall, when the next drawing in of air was sharp, violent and shook me awake. There was a tapping sound, not in the cellar, elsewhere, getting closer. A great wailing cacophony mounted to a deafening pitch.

I took the steps three at a time on the way up, hurtled to the front door, locked it quickly and sped away in the car as if my life depended on it.

The slates are lifted up and down,
That hang against the wall

X

[1981 - The same night]

The crescendo in the schoolhouse cellar died away and
the tapping sound could be heard again, this time diminishing into the distance. Mabel Hinde stole away
from her back door, looking around intently for witnesses. She was unseen. Darkness had descended suddenly that evening and Mabel was determined to make
good use of it. Making swift progress up Church Hill,
past the churchyard, then across country, through the
white iron fence that surrounded the cricket ground.
Mabel's coat was wide open and flew behind her as she
marched resolutely over the carefully manicured surface. She disappeared into the undergrowth, moist, cold
and tangled, and beyond into the trees that lined the
abandoned railway. Deftly scrambling down one bank
and keeping her momentum to scale the opposite one,
she arrived at the new cemetery. Mabel tramped even
more determinedly, no, maliciously, over the graves until she reached the far wall. She knew which spot she
was aiming for. Leaning over and smiling, she took one

final look around before rolling over the wall. This was the site of the Volta Tower. Her last great triumph. What remained was a mound, little more. A scrub wasteland with just one or two cut stones protruding from the surface.

Mabel climbed to the summit of the small mound and surveyed the site. She was immensely pleased, as she always was here; it renewed her when she was feeling weak. The other thing that reinvigorated her was coming to, she could sense her. Nearing, drawn as she was to this site, this testimony to their power.

The Dutch Doll emerged from the Dolben Crypt at the West end of the church. It was dull-eyed, seemed half alive. This was a wonder in itself, but to anyone who had seen it at its liveliest, at its most destructive, its' current state was almost sleeping. It skittered mechanically across the churchyard, across the road, before following Mabel's route to the tower site. Reaching the cemetery wall, its hand, placed on the top stone, was enveloped by a fleshy, wrinkled and veined one, that clasped it with delight. All at once Mabel swung the living wooden effigy high over the wall and into her arms, where she held it like a baby. The doll at first flopped loosely in her embrace, then struggled slightly, as a child would, to be put down. They held hands, the doll coming more to life, its features becoming more rounded, its eyes brightening. Mabel was in rapture as the ground started to rumble, then shake more noticeably, until finally the outline of the Volta Tower began to take shape around them. It was an immense structure, the main cylindrical tower over one hundred feet high, with patterned light and rust coloured stones, gargoyles towards the top and cruci-form slits in the castellated crown. There was a more customary house adjoining the tower, first on two storeys, stepping down to one, almost the same length as the tower was high. Each ghost stone laid itself meticulously in its rightful place, until the whole edifice, shining and translucent, surrounded the two exterminating angels, still holding hands at the base of the tower.

Within the phantom building, this reconstruction conjured up by Mabel and the Dutch Doll for their own amusement, moved the form of a woman, Constance Harte, in middle age, except that this was a vision, not of middle-life, but of her last day on earth. She took shining steps down from midway up the tower and went into the annex, until she turned suddenly, as though disturbed by a sound. Ah, it was a knock at her door, she was heading for the front door. The tower's door was concealed from the world by mature trees. No one, unless they had a mind to go to the door themselves, could witness what happened.

Constance opened the door, cheerfully, with only the pleasant expectation that this might be the milkman, or the butcher's boy. Instead she found Mabel, in a dirty mackintosh, with hair scraped back. Constance's face dropped and she took a step back.

"Oh, its you", was all that she could say.

"Don't you think you can accuse me at my own door and not expect a return visit", Mabel said, with no pretence of good manners.

"You can't come and continue the slanging match here, don't think you can", Constance rebuked as bravely as she could. She went to shut the door, but Mabel was too quick for her, stepping into the doorway to prevent her.

"I think you'll find I can do anything I like", Mabel threatened.

"You killed him, didn't you?", Constance came right out with it. This called for a candid and blunt conversation, she thought, if only to settle in her own mind what had really happened. "Come on, there's no one else here - I know you did it."

"You know and I'll easily admit that I killed him, I'll make no bones about that", Mabel replied brazenly. "He was no husband to me, he didn't share my beliefs, was beginning to object to some things that were going on in 'his' house and I was having none of that. He needed to be calmed down. Once I had him calmed, he seemed superfluous."

"So you poisoned the poor man?"

"Oh, I had help." Mabel looked around by the porch as if looking for something.

"From who?"

"From our friend in the cellar", answered Mabel with high drama. Constance was visibly shaken by the thought, even the slightest allusion, to the thing that invaded her dreams. Especially at church, although it brought a sense of relief in many ways, that the Dutch Doll was subdued, the horror was brought back home. Constance always averted her eyes from the back wall of the church, always took a front pew, rarely attended church unless she had to. She decided to go each week to chapel instead, to avoid the unhappy reminder, the lurking menace that she still felt when she set eyes upon it, or was in the presence of it. The same hairs were rising now, at the thought (was it just the thought?) of being near the doll.

"But h-h-how could the...um...doll help you - it can't get free of the church, it can't get free", Constance repeated, in the hope that the repetition would make it true.

"Can't she get free? Oh, you'd be surprised. Tied up in the church, yes, but if I hold my breath, and go in there and wriggle her free, I can get her out occasionally. I can warm her up and bring her back to life. And she breathes life into me." Mabel looked out around the porch again, "Come on, my love", she called.

The doll, walking very slowly, stiffened as she was by her confinement, appeared in the doorway. Constance screamed.

"Now, Now", Mabel spat through clenched teeth, with concentrated excitement, "this won't hurt a bit, not if you don't struggle". She put her hand over Constance's mouth and pushed her deeper into the house. The doll followed, pulling the door behind it.

The phantom, dream-like Constance fell back against the foot of her stairs. The very real, very much of this time Mabel and Dutch Doll were on her before she could take breath. They were re-enacting their murder, celebrating the final grinding under heel of Miss Connie Harte. Mabel held down a struggling Constance and beckoned to the doll, which was tugging at Constance's shoe, to give her something. The doll produced a sopping handkerchief that Mabel snatched and put over her old enemy's mouth. The struggling intensified for a brief moment, then poor Constance was finally subjugated. She was transfixed, rigid with eyes still open, still showing the full terror of her predicament. Once their victim was paralysed and an ectoplasmic web slowly enveloped her, Mabel and the doll withdrew, a look of wild triumph in both faces. Then they were outside again, in the cold night lit by the shining, effervescent tower. And they began to incant:

"Hell is the cauldron and the devil is the spoon", over and over, to no particular tune, but with growing intensity, until the pitch became so harsh, the din so abrasive, that stones began to shift. Small clouds of dust and tiny stones crumbling first, becoming a steady shower of debris, as Mabel and the Dutch Doll retreated, walking backwards and continuing with their shrieked spell. The upper-most battlements waved, like wheat in the wind and a large piece broke away, thumping through a slate roof below. Then another, followed by a dislodged gargoyle hurtling towards the ground. Finally an horrific implosion, a collapsing pack of cards, accompanied by an earthquake rumbling, which lasted long after the final stone could be seen falling into the rising dust cloud. Mabel and the doll rounded off with one last "Hell!" in unison, as they realised they'd done what they'd set out to do. Turning to each other, they started to giggle, louder and louder. The dust cleared and a mound of rubble came into view, the porch almost the only thing still standing and the whole scene resounding to the sound of their hysterical laughter.

All this appeared in a dream to George Mason, as he sat in his armchair dozing. He saw everything, crystal clear; the construction and demolition of the ethereal tower and the replay of the stifling of Constance. Shaking himself awake, he sat for a moment in a cold sweat, the light of his reading lamp shining against his right temple. He took two deep breaths to compose himself and looked warily around. As the familiar untidiness unfolded before him, George regained his composure, looked at the page in his book, looked at his bookmark, an old postcard of the Volta Tower, and smiled. 'A simple remembrance dream' he explained to himself, 'embellished by an overworked imagination and a quarter bottle of whiskey'. Raising himself unsteadily to his feet, he made a careful inspection of his flat, turning on each light, checking each window and door before retiring. Unfortunately, George's visions did not end there.

It appeared that immediately he was asleep again, George was dreaming once more. His room turned into a cabin or a hold on a rocking ship, with all the pitching and rolling and creaking and streaming water that comes with a storm at sea. There were barrels and folds of sail and coils of rope, lit by a violently swinging lantern. He himself was laying there in a bed in this place and he knew it to be a ship called The Volta.

Into this scene entered, or more correctly fell, a sailor in breeches and rough suede jerkin. As far as George could tell, this was a very dark man, perhaps Greek or Italian, with rat tail hair and a long ragged beard. He had great orbs for eyes, made even more desperate by the severe rocking of the ship.

"Captain he says to go on deck - we see land", was as eloquent as his pidgin English would allow. Without waiting for an answer, he was tugging at George's shirt. It was a white shirt, George noted, not his pyjamas.

George complied, "I'm coming, I'm coming", he said, though not in his own voice.

He picked his way clumsily between the debris-strewn room. A pewter plate struck his shin and flew off to the far right corner, as he followed the seaman towards the hatch at far left. It was then he saw what the dream was hurtling towards: a vision of the Dutch Doll. Propped up in the corner, with a rivulet of water running from cap to nose to neck, to collar, snaking down bodice and skirt, it watched him. This vision magnified in his dream to fully articulate its repugnance. What gripped his heart most was not the doll's lively face, fully animated and fearful. George had heard of this before and was prepared for it. So, even though this horrified him, it was not the most horrifying aspect. What shocked him most, what generated a sound that shook like the brass section of an orchestra blasting into his ears, resonating down to his diaphragm, was that the feet were intact. The spindly ankles so often seen truncated, now possessed boots. Neat little lace ups, with perhaps fifteen pairs of eyes for the laces on each boot and at the back, a half inch heel. In shiny black. They moved. They clicked together twice. 'Once more to go home', thought George whimsically, thinking of Dorothy. Or perhaps not whimsy, more accurate to say hysteria. One black boot lifted off the deck and stepped towards him.

George shot up in bed and turned on his bedside light. He took a gulp of water and placed his glass down. With the same movement, he picked up the notebook that always lay by his side at night, ready to record half conscious inspiration or dream sequences. He noted down this one in single linked words, ending:

"Became aware instantly that there is connection btwn Volta the boat & Volta Tower. More than Dolben's death & remembrance. The collapse of Tower & sinking of ship both involved Dutch Doll."

After writing and the writing itself calming him down, George sank back against his headboard and began to doze. It was three in the morning by now; George heard his mantelpiece clock strike the hour in his semi conscious state. He was shook, as we all are from time to time, by that feeling of suddenly stepping off a curb stone into thin air. Only this time it was accompanied by a muffled smash. Shaken awake, George lifted his head. Oh, his aching neck, he thought, oblivious to the impending doom. Rubbing it and about to turn off his light, there was another sound, a crumpling of papers. No one could walk across George's sitting room floor in the dark without treading on paper. George took up his water glass and stepped out to the foot of his bed.

"What are you doing here!" George shouted, hoping to alert his neighbours and frighten his intruder. He already had an idea as to who was skulking around his flat. His suspicions were confirmed, when he began to make out the black shape of a woman with long hair and that something else that he expected to be with her. Yes, two eyes, like a cat's caught in headlights, shining at him.

"Mabel Freeman!" George uttered, using her maiden name, "Take that beast of yours and...."

But he had no time to finish. In a flash, Mabel's dark shape hurtled towards him, in a juddering glide as though on worn casters, arms outstretched before her. As her face came into the light, he could see a vacant stare, eyes open wide, lips parted. George threw his glass at her. It struck her cheek and drew blood and still she kept on coming. Her hands reached George's neck before his own could parry them. She grasped him by the windpipe and squeezed. George fell back onto his bed and Mabel followed, still clenching. George tried to pull her hands away but was prevented by something. Then he realised that the Dutch Doll was at his head, pulling both his hands up above him, then sitting on them, slapping her hands down in glee onto his forehead.

"Thought you could get the better of me, did you George?", hissed Mabel in his face. "Come around my house, meddling, eh? You'll never be any match for me. Not while I have the Dutch Doll. Not while we have the power in our bones." George gagged, gurgled and gasped, his eyes popping, his face red. "You never were much of a worry as a scaredy-cat boy and you've grown into a weak, cowardly man. Without your friends, you're defenceless."

Mabel pressed heavier, sitting on George's chest as she strangled him. Then there was the sound of someone else coming up the stairs, a number of people. Someone had called the police. Mabel and the doll, disturbed, leapt off George and deftly made their escape by the route they'd taken in: through the kitchen and down the fire escape.

"In here - he'll need an ambulance", was the last thing Mabel heard as she dropped off the final step. She and the doll picked their way through alleyways and gardens until they reached the spinney and knew they were not being followed.

"He'll not bother us anymore", she reach down, panting heavily, though grinning, caressing the Dutch Doll's chin.

I arrived early at George's flat, purely to reassure myself that he'd had a peaceful night, to find bedlam. Police crime scene tape blocking access, forensics team milling about and much confusion about the baker's shop below.

"I was just arriving for work, at about four-thirty" Jim the baker (and George's landlord) was saying for the fiftieth time already when I entered the shop, "and they were just taking him away. He looked a very sorrowful sight. Moaning and groaning, he was."

"Still conscious then?", I piped in from the back of a small crowd of eager village gossips.

"Yes, still with us", Jim answered, nodding an acknowledging nod in my direction, "but not long for this world, if I'm any judge of these things. He was wired up, grey and sweating."

Just then, WPC Griffiths came in and called me over. "We've been looking all over for you", she said. "George is over at the General and is asking to speak to you. Won't speak to anyone else - keeps saying he has something for you"

I followed a patrol car into the hospital grounds and was rushed to George's room. Inspector Vines was waiting outside. "Ah", he said, standing up, "we've got you then. The doctors say George's heart is under great strain. Can't guarantee he'll last the next twenty four hours. Insists on seeing you. Now, let me guide the questioning. Its very important that we get as much information from him about the perpetrators as we can." And with that, he opened the door for me.

George was lying, absolutely spent, on crumpled sheets. Blue lips beneath an oxygen mask, dark flickering eyes, swollen and streaked neck showing signs of a vicious crushing injury. A heart monitor feebly recorded a slow, irregular beat. He could see me enter and raised an eyebrow and a single finger in recognition. I went to sit down beside his bed and Vines took up position behind me.

"No - not him!" came George's muffled croak under the mask, a cloud of condensation marking his efforts.

"It's alright George", I said, "Inspector Vines won't interfere; you say what you need to say."

"My notebook..." George whispered.

"We have his notebook", Vines said. George let out a sigh.

He reached up to me, with extreme effort and I went down towards him. Hardly audible, he said: "The tunnel at the school end...it comes up in your cellar. There is...a door behind the old bookcase. I saw it...as a boy." He was struggling to keeping going, but at last he exhaled with "take the vicar..." Vines was straining to hear and, as George rattled, he reached over to push the buzzer. We came out of the room as vain attempts were made to save him.

"What was that, at the end?" Vines asked.

"Oh...something about Mabel. I couldn't make it out. Have you found her? Mabel? I'm sure - he was sure - that she's involved in all this."

"Yes, we've made a call on her, but she's not at home. We've got officers out searching - it won't be long. She can't have got far. And these dreams he's noting in his book", he showed me the entry in George's notebook, "all this about the Dutch Doll - what's Mabel Hinde's connection with that?

"I don't know Inspector", I replied, "perhaps she was involved in the...theft. But one thing's for sure: she's a very dangerous woman." I wandered off along the corridor.

"Don't leave the area without telling me", called Vines after me. He doesn't know what to think, I pondered.

"I'll be at home tonight", I shouted back.

I made straight for Nick's ward, slipped the duty nurse at a busy breakfast time and related the sad news to the vicar.

"Help me get out of here", Nick said, "I'm feeling much better this morning. And I'm needed back at home." We stuffed his belongings into a plastic bag.

And little children scream aloud,
When they the noises hear

XI

[1981, the same day]

With great haste, Nick, Louise and I gathered again at the vicarage. Nick appeared to be spurred on by the latest turn of events:

"We must act and act now against Mabel. We must seek her out and...and exorcise her, rid her of the demons that so obviously infest her. And if in finding her, we also discover the Dutch Doll, we must absolutely, categorically dispense with it."

"The police are searching for Mabel themselves, we've seen them everywhere. There's still a part of me that thinks we should let the authorities take over. This woman is capable of murder, we know. We've seen what she can do and you and I Nick have seen that the Dutch Doll is animated, possessed and probably at the root of it all", I said, beginning to feel somewhat defeated and worn out by the experience.

"And someone told me", Louise reported, "that they'd found blood on a glass at George's and a blood-stained blouse at Mabel's. So they have hard physical evidence that Mabel's involved. She's shot up the list of suspects for that and Emily's disappearance and the deaths of the two thieves - everything. The police will find and arrest her, without us needing to get anymore involved, without us having to sell them an implausible story about devil-worship or whatever."

"But if they discover her and arrest her and lock her up and throw away the key, that won't be the end to it", Nick argued. "She may be incarcerated, there may even be a slur of satanic ritual surrounding her, but there are no witchcraft laws, nothing to take it seriously. No priest will minister to her as she needs. And most important, there's a risk that the Dutch Doll will stay out there, will continue to wreak havoc alone, or worse, will seek out a fresh supporter."

"I need to be with Emily and I'm not putting her in any danger, she'll be staying away with me until all this is over." Louise said emphatically. "I'm not convinced I want my husband put in any danger either", she added, turning to Nick. I was lost in thought, completely ambivalent.

"I can't do without him, I'm afraid Louise", said Nick consolingly, "if I could avoid involving you, I would. And although I'm determined and mentally, spiritually strong, I've only just discharged myself from hospital and I'm still physically weak. I'm relying on you to help, because you're the only people who understand the seriousness of all this, the only ones who won't now sneer at the ghost stories." He was almost pleading now. "Even if I were to go to the church authorities, they would take a lot of convincing that we needed 'back-up' to repel the evil one in this sleepy little village."

Louise turned back to me. "What do you think?" half imploring me to do something, half concerned for me, ultimately not helping me to decide.

"Looking logically", I said, "and I at least have to look at the cold facts as I see them. If there is a danger, and I know it to be a real, tangible danger, then I couldn't live with the thought of other people, other children, being at risk having just withdrawn from the problem, absolving myself from all responsibility. I do it with a heavy heart, because I also have a responsibility to my wife and child, but I will help you however I can vicar."

"Thank you", sighed Nick, relieved. "I will look after him, Louise, don't worry. We must act now, in the daylight." Turning to me: "You and I need to go up into the church."

It was a crisp, bright autumn morning, with the last of the frost burning off, as we crossed the vicar's garden to the church. The clear sky and perfect clarity made me feel much more secure, though Nick was in need of insurance.

"We must be armed to the teeth. Not with guns or knives. With weapons of faith." Once in the church, he opened his small haversack at the font and lined up five small bottles. He said a short prayer over the water and asked me to fill them. As I watched the bubbles erupt to the surface, Nick disappeared into the vestibule at the rear of the church, returning with a well thumbed church bible and a small jar. "Christening ointment; what we use to make the sign of the cross on their foreheads", he explained cheerfully. Gathering these armaments up in his bag, the vicar slung them over his shoulder. "Now", he said, "poor George told you that there was an unexplored piece of the tunnel network, at your house."

"Yes, must have been beyond the collapsed part that we saw. He said it joined my house in the cellar behind the bookcase. Its a massive piece of furniture. Always been with the house, because its too big to get out. Must have been built down there."

"Well, we'll go and see what's behind it."

Once at the house, I hesitated and explained my experience the day before when I'd felt a breathing in the cellar and the noise that swelled up to a deafening pitch.

"Just as they described the hauntings in the eighteen twenties", Nick said, "they were known as 'the noises' hereabouts. They said that three girls caused them. It appears now that they were falsely accused. Don't worry. There are two of us. We've only been attacked when we've found ourselves alone. And we have our arsenal", he smiled, patting his bag.

All the same, I let him lead the way down into the cellar.

Once on the cold stone slabs, Nick and I took a closer look at the bookcase. "It, as you say, must have been built in stages and brought down. It's a formidable chunk of furniture. Mmm, let's get to it." His business-like manner made me feel slightly more comfortable. "Blimey! It feels as though this hasn't been moved for some time."

"Probably not for nearly fifty years", I replied, "Since the murder of that girl, when George was a boy."

"Terrible business. I didn't realise that she'd been found down here."

"Apparently so. They don't tell you that sort of thing when they sell houses." We heaved together, shifting the huge bookcase half an inch and bringing with it half a century of accumulated grime. "If we can just get some purchase behind it - pushing is bound to be easier than pulling", I suggested. We eased the massive carcass inch by inch, until I was finally able to get a shoulder behind, then it got easier. With three more grunted efforts, the bookcase was at a forty-five degree angle to the wall.

"There is a door!" I exclaimed. Nick rummaged in his bag and produced two torches. The fresh batteries shone stark yellow light on the view. There was a padlock on the latch, which I reached over and rattled. I rubbed it with my thumb and yanked it hard. "Stuck fast", I said, "even if we had the key it would be impossible to move it; looks seized up with rust." I examined my red thumb. "I'll go and get my toolbox".

I bounded up the stairs and returned, in less than a minute, to find Nick on his knees. "What are you doing?" I asked.

"Saying a few words", Nick whispered back. "Whilst you were gone, I felt something - the sort of thing you did - shifting air, a noise. A sort of orchestral tuning up, steadily gaining pace."

"Yes, that's it", I said. Opening my toolbox: "Now, sledgehammer or hacksaw?"

"Hammer, I think."

After three deft blows, the lock was still intact. With the fourth swing, it fell away, still intact and the latch itself removed from the door. It swung open slightly. Nick stuck his torch in. Brick lined walls. He pulled the door open more to reveal a rubbish strewn floor.

"Careful now", said Nick, "and stick close." He entered the tunnel cautiously and trod as though on egg shells.

"This is in a hell of a mess", I said.

"Yes, and a very recent mess too. These newspapers are recent. Look -", Nick crouched down, "- these chocolate wrappers aren't fifty years old. They've obviously been holed out here." He reached into his bag for one of the bottles of holy water and sprinkled it on the ground and said a short prayer: "May the Lord Jesus bless this place and bring peace and safety to all who walk here."

A sound of disturbed rubble made us cock our ears. Nick held out his hand to silence me. Another scrape of brick against brick.

"Come on!" Nick whispered and we lumbered as fast as we could along the tunnel. Barely twenty yards on, a pile of rubble appeared to block our way. Then we saw a puff of brick dust...and...yes! At the top, a sensible brown shoe disappeared from sight. Nick clambered up the pile as fast as he could and pointed his light through the gap. He looked back at me in horror.

"They're through here - both of them!" Nick said. "I'm going through. You hold onto my leg and come through with me. I don't want to be left alone on the other side for one moment." He edged his way through, dragging his bag at his side. I held onto him as requested and followed him through the orifice. The gap was only ten inches high and three feet long before it opened out again. I fell headlong down the other side, scraping my elbow.

"You alright?" asked the vicar, seeing my wince. But he didn't wait for my nod before proceeding down the tunnel. We trotted on until we reached the familiar intersection.

Nothing.

"Not left", I said, "that's where the water is. And not straight ahead - we know the exit at the Bell Inn is closed. So my bet's on right - back to the crypt."

"I'm with you", Nick said. We made our way in the curved incline towards the church. On reaching the black grill, Nick again paused and listened. "There's no sound at all", Nick whispered, "surely if they'd come back this way, they couldn't have opened the grate, closed it again and made their way to the surface?"

"I don't know", I said, "lets just have a quick look."

Back at the Girl's School, Louise was dropping by with Emily, oblivious to the drama unfolding below.

"You stay here Emily", Louise instructed, "While I get some more clothes. Do you want anything?"

"My giraffe", Emily asked, thinking of her night-time comfort. Then the little girl was left in the entrance hall. It only took a second for a breeze to pick up about Emily's fine long hair. Something took her attention. In the old laundry passageway. She could hear her name being called. Gently, in a sing-song girl's voice, "Emily...Emily...". She followed the beckoning sound, down the passage bathed in late morning light, through the open cellar door, down the steps into an enveloping gloom.

There at the bottom, very calm and oblivious to all danger, Emily came to Mabel and the Dutch Doll. The doll had returned to its reposed, statue state, leaning against the old woman. Mabel stood, with her hand on the doll's shoulder, breathing heavily and smiling sweetly.

"Ah, Emily, there you are. We've been looking for you", said Mabel.

"Was it you calling my name?", asked Emily, not at all perturbed.

"Yes, we wanted to see you", replied Mabel, nice as pie. "Do you remember us from the other night?"

"Yeees", Emily drew out the word. Then, recalling, screwed up her forehead into a frown, "it was you who scratched my ankles." She took a step backwards.

"No, no Emily, I don't think you remember it properly", Mabel stepped forward, leaving the doll, which remained standing. "No, you scratched yourself on the brambles and the doll and me, we helped you get back home." Emily remained confused looking, as Mabel ingratiated further, "and we said we'd teach you a rhyme."

"Yes."

"Would you like to learn it now? You'll like it - it will make everything seem so much better." Mabel drew nearer and Emily felt suddenly much more at ease.

At the crypt, Nick and I were peering over the edge of the upper cavity, out over the churchyard towards the road.

"I'm pretty sure they didn't come this way", I said, "or, if they did, they shut up very quickly after themselves and they're long gone."

"If they didn't come this way, could they have got out via one of the other tunnel branches; the stream conduit or the pub?" Nick wondered.

"We didn't check either branch before coming this way - they could still be down there!" I said, already dropping back down into the coffin filled lower pocket of the crypt. We quickly slipped into the tunnel again and wound down to the subterranean crossroads.

"Which way now?" Nick asked.

"Well, they could be miles away by now, but we should check the two branches that we haven't explored so far today", I suggested, striking out towards the blocked Bell Inn exit. We reached the closed door, as immoveable as the last time we saw it, as dead an end as before.

"The stream then", Nick said. And we headed back. Just before the intersection, we began to hear a sound that we'd both heard before. A growing orchestral moan, increasing in pitch and volume. We stood transfixed, looking, listen down each tunnel.

"It's back at the schoolhouse - they're back at the house!" I shouted, running along the tunnel that we'd entered by this time, almost having to push against the terrible sound, like a high wind. Amid the other-worldly noise, there leapt an ear splitting child's scream.

In the cellar, Emily was being embraced by Mabel. The Dutch Doll, slowly becoming more animated, grasped Mabel's skirt with one hand and Emily's cardigan with the other. The scroll and book that it held when still, were tucked into its little black jacket. All three were reciting that stanza, heard before, over a terrible and ominous din. Wind was rushing around and around as they stood, as though in the eye of the storm.

And this is how Nick and I came upon them, having to clamp hands on our ears for the last tunnel section, the noise being so unbearable. As we stepped sideways from behind the bookcase, it was as though an electronic circuit was broken; the wind stopped in an instant and the noise died away, just its resonance, like the tone after the striking of a bell, remained for a second or two. The three companions stayed huddled together for a moment to utter the last line of their rhyme: "...devil is the spoon!". Mabel realised that we were upon her and pivoted on one heel, sending Emily and the doll careering off in different directions. She winced - no - hissed at us. The vicar fumbled in his sack and whipped out his bible, reading from Revelation:

"And upon her forehead was written, '*Mystery, Babylon the Great, the mother of harlots and abominations of the earth*'. And I saw the woman drunken with the blood of the saints..." He got no further. Mabel screeched, grabbed Emily's arm and made for the cellar steps. Just as she did, Louise appeared in the doorway at the top.

"What's happening down there", she yelled, "Emily, are you there?"

Mabel turned into the cellar again as Nick and I advanced on her. But we hadn't reckoned on the Dutch Doll. It was behind us in a flash and pawing at our calves. The shock and not insignificant pain distracted us for the time that Mabel needed to pass us. By that moment, Louise too was down in the cellar and calling out for Emily, who was still held by the arm by Mabel Hinde. Emily wore a worryingly far-away, sleepwalker's expression. A mother's protective instinct is so strong that, even though Louise had not seen the Dutch Doll in action before, even though the sight was alarming and nothing short of pandemonium, she did not hesitate to leap forward. Louise grabbed Emily's arm, the one that Mabel also held. She tried to prize Mabel's hand off, but without success. Then Mabel - seeing that Nick and I had freed ourselves from the Dutch Doll, which had scuttled off like a scorpion into the hole of the tunnel - she too backed off towards the tunnel door. In desperation and realisation that today's game was up, she finally hurled Emily at the three of us. I caught my daughter roughly, but sprawled backwards and took the vicar with me. Louise stood in utter shock for a moment, before helping us up.

"Emily, Emily, are you alright?", she said, taking Emily by both shoulders and giving her a gentle, earnest shake. "Emily!"

Emily shook her head and grumbled "Uh? What? What do you want?", as if waking from a deep sleep.

"It's mum, Emily, are you hurt?"

"My head hurts a little bit mum", Emily answered, "Did you get my Giraffe?"

"She's alright", Nick said, almost callously. Because he had an urgent preoccupation. "Let's get after them", he said to me, tugging me back into the tunnel. I didn't know what to do. Except I knew that my wife and daughter were not apparently harmed and not in danger. The source of any potential danger were in retreat. As long as I was between my family and the enemy, I was content enough. Nick had a look of intense determination that I'd never seen in anyone before, absolutely full of energy, amazing for a man confined to his hospital bed two days before.

"Quicker!" he tugged at me, as we scrambled again to the narrow section. Down the other side and towards the intersection. This time, Nick saw which path our adversaries took. "They're definitely heading up to the church this time!" he said. We veered right and up towards the crypt. I just caught sight of the doll and Mabel up ahead. The latter moving in a swift stooping lumber, the former almost being dragged along. We could see them reaching the metal grate at the tunnel end that joined the crypt.

"Here's our chance!" said Nick, highly excited. But he was almost halted in his tracks, as the two up ahead swung the grill open and shut again with a heavy bang, which was the only thing that betrayed its weight. "I can't bel...", Nick was lost for words. As we reached the gate ourselves, we saw the wicked pair tampering with the contents of one of the coffins, the one on the floor that we had seen so badly disturbed before. As we pushed at the grate, finding it slow and hard-going, they scaled the stacked coffins to reach the half open grill to the upper chamber. We were very lucky that they didn't think to pull this piece of ironwork back into place - that would have as good as sealed this exit for us. Once squeezed into the coffin filled chamber, we used the stacked caskets too and were quickly out into the sunlight of the upper chamber. Mabel was already over the railings, seemingly in one vault, and beckoning the doll over as she looked frantically to her left and right.

I grabbed hold of the doll's legs as it tried to lever itself out over the railings. It was surprisingly warm and rough - not like a table leg; like the branch of a tree. It tried to shake me off, but I took a firmer hold. I could feel myself almost being lifted from the ground. How could this little three foot manikin contain such power? When it realised that I wasn't letting go and Nick was behind me reaching for another bottle of his holy water, it turned on me like a wild cat, baring teeth that I hadn't seen before, didn't know it possessed. They were small yellow things, feline too. The doll thrashed out at me with its razor fingers, catching me above the left elbow. The intense stinging and colouring of my shirt, seeping red, made me loosen my grip. One last struggle and the doll was free, leaping over the black iron railings. But not before the vicar had flung his water at it, causing a puff of steam. Mabel pulled it away a few more yards and threw her coat tails onto its frock, as though she were smothering a fire, then she picked up the doll and slid around the North side of the church. Nick and I clambered over the railings, more heavily and less athletic than the unprepossessing agility of our quarry. By the time we made it round the buttress corner of the church, we could see no movement, no sign of the Dutch Doll or Mabel.

"Where in heaven's name?" Nick said, astounded.

"Let's carry on", I encouraged. Without luck, we searched the vicarage garden and outhouses before circling the church twice more. "It's no use", I said finally, "they could be anywhere - we've lost them again. I must get back to Louise and Emily."

"Of course, of course", Nick said, "you go on. I'll secure things at this end", tapping the crypt iron railings, "and I'll be over in a few minutes."

As I marched double quick back to the old schoolhouse, Nick started to climb the railings once more, before a sudden realisation and smile passed across his face and he shook his head at his own foolishness. Reaching down in his bag, he found a large iron key and proceeded to unlock the railing gate. He needed to investigate something.

Down in the lower chamber, Nick flicked on his torch. It was still midday outside, but very little light penetrated down there. He went straight over to the most damaged coffin, the one belonging to Thomas Dolben the Younger. The whole thing had caved in. No, not *in*. Thomas himself was just bone. His skull looking upwards, with a few wisps of red hair, his lower jaw detached and fallen somewhere out of sight. Nick looked more closely between the ribs and could make out brassy objects in the dusty floor of the casket - a buckle and some buttons perhaps. Nick looked again at the lid;

splintered outwards from the very top to two thirds of the way down.

Back at my house, the vicar called on me to give his theory. But not before hearing from me on the strange affliction that had visited Emily.

"She's unusually...guarded, is the best word for it, I suppose", I said. "When I got back, she was in her bed, still there now with Louise...She is very distracted, almost trance-like. Not really with us. She doesn't appear to be unwell, but I'd say she's been psychologically damaged in some way. All she says - and she's said it a few times - is 'not if you know what to do'"

"I was afraid of that", the vicar said, "They've got hold of her in some way. If we're to free Emily properly, we need to carry on doing what we set out to do - seek out and destroy the doll. They seem to be able to slip through our fingers all too easily. We must approach it from another angle - try to second guess their motive; try to find a weakness. They were worrying around that coffin in the crypt just now, did you see? My strong feeling is that the doll came back to this village with Thomas Dolben and was buried with him. Maybe it was some sort of ships mascot, or a sailor's carving. This is certainly borne out by poor George Mason's last dream - you said you saw it noted in George's book, which Inspector Vines showed you at the hospital?" I nodded. "He dreamt about being in a ship in a storm and about being in someone else's shoes and that someone else encountering the Dutch Doll there. Well, he was somehow reliving Thomas Dolben's last hours, aboard a ship called the Volta, off the West Coast of Africa. In 1824. He was drowned."

"What was he doing in West Africa a hundred and fifty years ago?" I wondered out loud.

"What was any 'entrepreneur' doing in Africa then - making money on the back of the trade in people - even if it were illegal by then", Nick wrinkled his nose in disgust. "That might just be it. He was involved in a terrible cursed business. Justification, or a reason, for him to have a curse laid upon him. In the form of the thing that was washed up with him. Something that perhaps his relatives here in England thought of as a memento of Thomas' ship. But something that carried with it a disease that would be infecting people for centuries to come", (he nodded in the direction of the room where Emily lay), "- I'm afraid to say. It took no time in freeing itself from its internment and began to wreak havoc, one hundred and fifty years ago. The Dutch Doll".

XII

[1824]

Thomas Dolben the Younger lay in his coffin, perfectly preserved. When the shipping agents wrote to say that they'd acquired the body, they said *"the bodie has been dried to parchment, by the unrelenting and extremely warm climate & by the funereal practice of that climate."* And so, a full three months after his demise, his desiccated husk came back to England. With him (actually partly inside his exposed abdominal cavity) was the Dutch Doll.

"Not the sort of thing that can be viewed by my dear wife?" Sir Thomas Dolben the Elder asked. He was with the vicar of the day, the Reverend Samuel Paul, who was the great grandfather of the village vicar of the nineteen thirties. Thomas was a corpulent, red faced country squire, dejected, thoroughly extinguished, by the death of his eldest son. They were sitting in the elegant blue drawing room of the Hall.

"Not sir, something that I would recommend", said the Reverend. He was full of his own self importance, a very powerful man in his own right, rarely playing second fiddle to anyone. Only to Sir Thomas, would he submit or defer to. And this only grudgingly. "As one who has lain eyes on your poor son's sorry remains, I can only say that yours and Lady Elizabeth's feelings are better spared further injury. Your minds are better dwelt on happy memories of the sweet, fresh-faced youth that we all knew so well and were so fond of."

"Quite so", Sir Thomas said, reflecting. "Well, then Reverend, if the funeral arrangements are all taken care of....?"

"Actually sir, there is just the matter of the figurine that travelled with young master Thomas."

"A Dutch Doll, you say?"

"Yes, a figurehead of the Volta, do you think?"

"Possible, quite possible, though I never saw the vessel. My son wrote very fondly of the ship and the experience of sailing with her, but, strange to say, did not mention any figurehead. Certainly not a heathen African carving. So, as we can do nought but assume the figurine was carved by a Christian, blessed as the ship was launched and came to be with my boy when he breathed his last, it is only right that this last surviving connection with his beloved ship remain with him.

"Of course sir, I'll ensure its taken care of", and with this, the Reverend rose from his chair, performed a shallow perfunctory bow and departed.

Two days after the funeral, the coffin being placed in the family vault, the quiet inactivity of the chamber was broken on the stroke of four o'clock in the morning. First, a muffled bump, then scratching, and finally frantic industry from within Thomas's casket. Still no visible sign of disturbance. In any case, no witnesses; no one even awake within a quarter of a mile. But if you had been there, sitting quietly in the corner, you would have seen a single splinter of coffin lid burst up, and another. Another larger piece before a brown finger poked through and circled around, as if sniffing the air. Then a short, fierce barrage from within, resulting in a larger hole from which full purchase could be gained. If you were brave enough to endure this, you would then have seen a concerted wrenching of the wood until it finally gave way and the Dutch Doll sat up, looking swiftly left and right with maniacal stare. Yet the chamber was empty, save for long dead members of the Dolben Family.

Sensing it was free and unwatched, the doll rose to its feet and stepped out, shaking splinters from its boots. It surveyed the crypt first from its sedentary vantage point, then by skipping swiftly around, running its hands along the three stacked coffins to the side of Thomas's, breathing in cold air from the back grate in the corner. It was this that attracted most attention and before long, the doll tugged at the wrought iron. With surprising ease, the grate gave way and was with equal freedom brushed back into place. The doll found itself in the catacombs beneath the old part of the village. Clean and unsullied for now, these tunnels were unused and largely unheard of during those times. The Dutch Doll walked majestically down to the intersection and breathed in through twitching nostrils. In one direction, it could detect water, in another, ale and in the third…Oh, this way was by far the most intriguing. Lavender, rosewater and human musk. The undeniable aroma of small girls. The doll raced along to the small door that stood between it and domination.

From inside the cellar, all was calm. The enormous bulk of the bookcase covered one end of the room, though less darkened by age than we've seen it since. And it began to shift. Not with any amount of grating or noise; with a gradual sliding arc until there was just enough room, barely two thirds of a foot, for the manikin to sidle in. It stepped on tiptoes across the cold stone floor and crawled on hands and feet up the steps, its face inches from each rise. Reaching the penultimate step with its nose, it paused and, settling down for a moment, scratched something in tiny neat letters into the face of the step. Nodding in appreciation of its handiwork, the doll proceeded to gently open the door at the top. It had no lock at that time. Again, taking time to sense or smell something in the air, it followed the passage around to the back stairs, along the rear corridor and up further to the girl's dormitory. There it stood outside the door, invoking from within itself, or perhaps from another, far superior force, a sort of aural bedlam. Best described as a slowly mounting dreadful sound, crashing of metal, the murdering of instruments. This sound stirred the three eldest girls, who were also the ones closest to the door.

Maria Hacksley, Sarah Durden and Hannah Randall were woken by the terrible din and had enough time to realise it was not a dream and to look to each other, indeed to go to each other for comfort, before the noises suddenly stopped. This equally alarmed them. Maria, the brightest of the three, said:

"Must've been a milk churn rolling down the road, or a....", but before she could conjecture further, she was silenced by scuffling. Then a sharp rap at the door, then the latch lifted slowly from the catch. The girls let out ear-splitting screams, which woke the whole house.

Miss McAlister, the headmistress, was on the scene within a minute, in long white night-coat and long plaited pony tail. She looked in at the girls, saw the three who were the centre of attention and demanded an explanation.

"Awful noises Miss", was all Sarah could blurt out between sobs.

"And something was trying to get us!", added Hannah.

"A lot of nonsense - why, do you not think that if someone was trying to get into your room, that I would not have passed them on the way up. Not a living soul is in this house, save for the ones that should be; you and I. Now get back to sleep and no more of it!"

"Its not the *living* souls that need concern us!" whispered Hannah to the other two, once the door was closed again.

The noises continued unabated for the next three nights, as the Dutch Doll's forays became bolder and bolder. It even started to slip the latch and eye up the three girls before summoning its demonic discord. It could quite easily gauge the effect it was having on the vulnerable, innocent creatures. As rumours circulated around the village, Miss McAlister sought the advice of the Reverend Paul.

"The three girls are quite insistent, one could say adamant, that the noises they hear are genuine. Yet I have not heard a pin drop, have not seen anything that has disturbed me. They, on the other hand, are extremely agitated."

"Would you go as far as to say the three young ladies are hysterical? Perhaps caught up in their own imaginings?", the vicar asked.

"They appear to have their full faculties sir, though I do feel, I'm sorry to report, that they are conjuring up mischief for themselves. I use the word 'conjure' in its most innocent guise, you understand", said Miss McAlister regretting the insinuation. It had been less than fifty years in this county since the last witch was burnt.

"I would venture to suggest that you use the word wisely, Miss", the Reverend Paul took the opportunity to capitalise, "and I will use this Sunday's sermon to remind these girls and all those in the village inclined to subject themselves to similar fancies, that no-one will gain from dabbling in the dark side, any more than the devil himself."

Maria, Sarah & Hannah sat timidly in their third row pew, staring at their shoes, as the vicar threatened fire and brimstone and the full wrath of God on those who seek pleasure or power from the use of witchcraft. This grave warning from the pulpit however, could not silence the three girls and could not help the panic from spreading among the simple country folk. On the contrary, the village saw an escalation in 'occurrences'. The noises and the girls' reaction to them woke neighbours. Many villagers reported an eerie whining, moaning, screeching sound that stirred them from their beds and made them feel most uncomfortable in their spirits. James Munns, a carter, was leading his horses from the field to the farmyard before sunrise one morning, when he saw a girl run across the road. Only it was close enough not truthfully to be mistaken for a girl. Feelings were running so high and rumours so wild that James felt no hesitation, was not shy to share the story of his sighting with his fellow labourers and fellow drinkers at the Bell. The visits to the girls in the schoolhouse became more brazen too.

On the second Saturday night since its first appearance, the Dutch Doll did something designed to terrorise the girls that it knew were within its grasp. It did not generate the noises this night, but slipped unhindered and unheard, from the catacomb hideaway up to the girls' room. It was the dead of night. A very still, calm night, cloudy, with no discernable moon and consequently very dark. Pitch. The only light in the bedroom was the faint red glow, the dying embers of the small fireplace. Even the door, prone to creaking as it opened, appeared oiled by an unnatural substance. So the doll found itself at the foot of the large bed that the three girls shared. Maria's head was at the foot of the bed. She was sandwiched between Sarah and Hannah, who slept on the edges, the right way around. The Dutch Doll was delighted to have the girls at such close proximity. It positioned itself inches from Maria's sleeping face and began intoning its satanic couplet. The words weevilled into Maria's ears, insinuated themselves into her head. And as the doll lullaby'd the noxious rhyme, it stroked Maria's hair. It was this that made the young girl sit up with a start. She saw a black shape by the bed and thought it to be one of the girls. She put out her hand to identify the interloper, only to find her wrist seized by a clamp, not of warm flesh, but by something harder, denser, colder. Maria let out a scream. The clamp let go. Girls were stirring in the room and at the far end, furthest from the door, one plunged a candle into the embers of the fire to ignite it. As she and the others drew closer to Maria's bed, on which Maria herself was trembling and sobbing and tugging at the blankets, they all saw the doll at the door. All were struck dumb and stuck to the spot. The Dutch Doll stood there in the flickering light, quite amazed that it was surrounded by this many living creatures, though not at all alarmed. It took a steady look around, into every face, smiled and said:

"Search ye the scriptures, girls", and chuckling to itself, opened the door - which creaked this time - and was gone.

On this occasion too, the doll appeared to Miss McAlister, who passed it along the rear passage. The doll, quite brazen by now, smiled the same smile as it sped past. The headmistress threw herself back against the wall, dropped her candle, which went out. She ran, faster than she ever had, up to the girls' dormitory. That night she didn't admonish them. First thing the following morning, she took her new found belief, sufficiently shrouded as it had to be to protect her position, to the vicar.

"I am becoming", she said to him, "to be more convinced than I once was, that the three girls we discussed previously are actually bound up in devilish activities. Whether they are caused by, or act upon, my charges, I cannot tell. But the noises persist and are real - the visions are shared, not just among the children, but...grown men and women too."

"Grown men and women have seen apparitions? Preposterous!" The Reverend Paul's good sense and his very stateliness prevented him from taking such supernatural events seriously. Yet he'd publicly acknowledged the workings of the devil before and couldn't, as the responsible citizen, perhaps the only man of good education in the village, ignore such rumours. "I'll vouch still, that this stems from nothing more than the fertile imaginations of your young charges. They've planted a diabolical seed that has taken hold in the simple minds of my parishioners, people who should be pitied for their vulnerability. I'll preach again this morning on the subject of fighting against the evil one, who invades an undisciplined soul and nests in the heart of a weak man."

"An admirable aim sir. I will listen most attentively. Though I have heard that villagers of some standing are also coming to believe in the stories", Miss McAlister put timidly, hoping that she would not be exposed as an undisciplined weakling.

"Of some standing? Who?", said the vicar, seeing then that Miss McAlister was not able - or willing - to divulge names. "Well, I must be left, as the one remaining *sober* person in the whole village, to dispel these stories. Good day madam - and be sure to secure the three miscreants a good view of the pulpit."

So the good Reverend Paul railed forth for a second Sabbath sermon, utterly condemning the practice of "collusion with horned and other beasts" and saving his best withering looks for Maria, Sarah and Hannah.

Thinking that this would see off any imp or goblin that Beelzebub could throw at him, the Reverend retired well satisfied. That same evening, he returned to the church to snuff out candles and took it upon himself to inspect the grave dug for a funeral he was holding the next day. It was at the West end of the church. He was relying on the last light of a yellow dusk to see by. He surveyed the work of George Locke, the gravedigger, a man on whom the Reverend Paul would rather not rely. Though, on this occasion, he found what he expected of his graves; a clean edge, a tidy mound of earth and - he peered in with intense concentration - the proper depth.

With no time to stand, the vicar felt a sharp push between his shoulder-blades. He tumbled headlong into the open pit, cart-wheeling and landing on his back with a jolt that shook him to the bone. Whether by shock, adrenalin, or determination not to sprawl in an ungentlemanly manner, he got his feet extremely quickly. There was a girl's deriding laugh.

"Who on God's earth are you to push me!" the vicar bellowed, expecting to hear a village girl crumble at the sound of his voice, or at least beat an escape. The girl did neither. The black, girl shaped thing came a little closer, until the vicar realised. In fact, he recognised the Dutch Doll from the time he'd seen it enclosed and nailed down inside Thomas Dolben's coffin. It mused over him, looking faintly ridiculous with his head at ground level. At first horrified, then dismissing with a smile his own foolishness, he yelled firmly, "Stay away from me, devil!"

To this, the doll sniggered again and said sweetly, "The scriptures priest, search them." It scooped a pile of earth and flung the wet clod straight into the Reverend Paul's face. As he reeled, falling back down to the bottom of the grave, more handfuls of earth rained down on the moaning vicar. Then stopped suddenly. Sir Thomas Dolben Senior, the old squire, had disturbed them.

"Are you injured sir?" the squire inquired, squinting in the half-light and recognising the vicar.

"Not physically Sir Thomas", said the reverend, acquiescing to his patron's offer of a hand out of the grave. They struggled and groaned in unison as the parson was unceremoniously dragged out.

"Thank you sir, you have saved me a very difficult task."

"But what led you to be in such an awkward location, did you fall? - the light is none too good."

"No sir, I'm afraid I was pushed, by a…by a girl, I think. Did you see a village girl running away, by chance?"

"A girl? No. I was intending to see you on my way home, about the occurrences that I've been hearing of, the ones you've been preaching a warning on."

"Yes sir", the vicar said, rubbing his knee, "It occurs to me that a certain amount of action, beyond preaching, may be required in this case."

The self same night, a young gentleman, by the name of Dexter, sat in the Bell Inn, jotting down a poem on the subject, which became widely circulated at the time.

Back at the schoolhouse, the three girls at the centre of this ancient intrigue, sat up in bed together, discussing the latest turn of events.

"I'm not closing my eyes tonight, I'll not set one foot out of bed, I'll not move an inch until morning", remonstrated a petrified Hannah, on the verge of tears.

"Don't be silly", said Maria, calm, somehow much more contented than the others. "The dolly doesn't wish us any harm. Can't do you no harm, in fact, not if you know…" and she wriggled her shoulders in comfortable superiority, "…listen, I'll teach you something to help keep her friendly. If you'll promise not to tell." Hannah and Sarah nodded fearfully - anything to prevent another night of terror.

Three hours later, as the church clock struck eleven, the three remained in their huddle - were still whispering. Miss McAlister had barricaded herself in her room and had instructed the girls to do the same. They had made a superficial attempt, bolting the dormitory door and scraping a chair or two to the door. Enough to satisfy their headmistress, who retreated to build her defences. But as soon as Maria heard her soft footsteps fading and checked that their fellow boarders were asleep, she silently returned the furniture to their places and slid back the bolt.

"Now we can wait for her", she said to Sarah and Hannah. They were at the very least bemused, at the very most still a little petrified. Maria was, of course, under a spell, subdued and mildly stupefied by it. You could see the intoxication in her half open eyes, her wane smile, her gentle voice. "As I said, there's nothing to be afraid of. You have me here and I know what to do. Just do as I do and you'll be released from your fears, you'll feel at one, at one with our lord."

"But shouldn't we go to the vicar for our Christian spirit, for him to lead us to salvation?" asked Sarah. "I'm worried that we're not going about this the right way - using the...the other thing. The Reverend Paul said that those who choose to walk with Satan must live with Satan in the bowels of hell for all eternity. That's an awful long time to be burning."

"What does he know?" said Maria scornfully, "he doesn't know what it feels like to be really lifted up. I do. I'm starting to get a warm feeling that radiates out from my middle and asks to touch others. That's why I'm asking you two to come with me. Of course, if you'd like I'll not help you and when the doll comes along, I'll just leave you to her...?"

Sarah and Hannah were showing signs of being convinced, were just about to remonstrate, to plead with Maria to help them, when a click at the door announced their expected visitor. Maria's eyes lit up with fascination, with anticipation; the other two girls had wide eyes borne of anxiety.

Once again, the Dutch Doll slinked into the room. It had taken the same route as previously; up through the catacombs and the cellar, past the headmistress's door. And now it stood, triumphant, in the threshold. It spoke, unabashed and at the height of its powers, in a clear young girl's voice:

"We're all here then, Maria. Are your friends ready to join us?"

Maria was dumbstruck, in awe, only able to nod eagerly.

"Then come", the doll encouraged, opening up its arms. The girls joined it, Maria in joyous haste, Sarah and Hannah with slower, more hesitant steps. But with Maria's help, they joined a circle of linking arms. The Dutch Doll began the familiar chant, the girls, one by one, joined in and the summoned cacophony mounted to a deafening pitch. First, the girls in the room were woken. They cowered under their sheets; a small group sat quivering in the corner. Miss McAlister was woken next. She knew exactly what must be happening, but was torn between her own fear and the need to protect her girls. She stood at her barricaded door for a full half minute, agonising. Finally, she could stand it no longer and tore at the furniture stacked at her door and, with poker in hand, leapt up to the girls' room. She looked on the scene completely aghast, then, enraged, made an animalistic yell. It didn't rise above the massive din still ongoing, but could at least be heard alongside. The doll and the girls stopped their chanting abruptly and turned to the teacher, poker raised above her hand.

As the noises died down, Miss McAlister said "You'll not have them!" and brought the poker down onto the doll's back. It toppled over like a skittle and in its last roll, managed to right itself again. With a speed that was almost beyond being visible, it weaved between the girls and the headmistress and was out of the room in two seconds. Miss McAlister chased it down the stairs and they both then discovered villagers in the hallway. Half the surrounding households had emptied onto the street, keen to see the latest occurrence and determined to put a stop to their disturbed nights.

"There's the creature!" one man shouted, taking a step back. Enough to let the doll slip past into the street. There, it ran into tens of men, women and children in their nightgowns, carrying lit torches and lanterns. Confused and disorientated above ground, the doll ran around in two wide circles, until it made out the tower of the church. It barged through a screaming pack of people and headed for the crypt. The Reverend Paul was coming down from the lych-gate and stopped, holding out a long staff in one hand, a large cape draped around him.

"Its you then - the devil's own! Outnumbered? Well, we'll not let you walk abroad again" and he took a brave swipe at the doll, as a group of villagers rounded the corner. The doll sidestepped him and ran through the lych-gate, followed closely by the Reverend Paul and five of the village men. They just reached the first tombstone in the churchyard in time to see the doll leap into the crypt.

"Let us go down Reverend...and sort this out once and for all", said one man.

"It needs weighing down in the mill pond, like the witch it is!" said another.

"No", said the Reverend, standing his ground, with his back to the iron railings and his hands raised up to halt the zealous huntsmen. "We will wait until the morn and go about this properly. Only one man can effectively banish beasts such as this and that man is the man of God that stands before you. Guard the entrance until the sunrise and I will return then." And with these proud words, the vicar swept off back to his bed.

The Reverend next appeared, as promised, as the sun's first rays spread long shadows across the dewy lawn of the vicarage. Before he'd reached the few steps to the churchyard, he saw Miss McAllister coming down them towards him.

"Ah, Reverend Paul sir, so very glad to catch you first. I need to tell you about the effect this monstrous thing has had on my three girls. They appear quite possessed. In a daze and unable to utter a coherent sentence."

"Is that so, my dear headmistress? Well, we must attend to that, but after our first piece of business today."

"Do you mean to destroy the thing sir?"

"At least disable, madam", said the reverend, brandishing his wood axe.

They reached the three remaining village men standing watch by the crypt entrance. "Capital, my faithful friends", said the vicar in an almost jovial tone, "it is good to see that you have lasted 'til morning. Tell me, has anything occurred?"

"No sir", answered the burliest of the three, "not a living soul nor a craven beast has passed, one way or t'other."

"Good. Then I must dispose of the wretched imp." With this, the vicar unlocked the iron gate and sat on the edge of the crypt chamber. "If you hear me holler, two of you must come down. Otherwise I'll be well." He dropped down into the first void, then without pausing into the lower one and out of sight.

Once on his feet and accustomed to the light, the vicar made a quick search of the tomb. He lightened immediately on the new coffin of Thomas Dolben Jnr, seeing that it was corrupted.

"Lord have mercy!" he whispered under his breath. A sight made him inhale sharply. Inside, finding comfort in the proximity to its last victim, was the Dutch Doll. The vicar could see the polished surface of its cap and collar. It was quite motionless, dead one would have said. The reverend seized it and pulled in one movement out onto the stone floor. It clattered, again solid and lifeless. As the vicar took his axe and raised it, he could feel a warmth rising in the object he was holding down with his right hand. As he brought down the first blow to its ankle, the doll's eyes came alive and movement returned to its fingers. But too late. The vicar had made three more well aimed blows and severed one foot. A piercing screech, like an owl, reverberated around the tomb. The doll began to recover enough movement to grasp the vicar's hands, as he was raining down chops on the other leg. The second foot rattled off into a corner, as the doll began to thrash. Finally, the Reverend Paul held his hand over the doll's mouth and recited the Lord's Prayer. As he did so, the doll's animation subsided and within a single minute, it had returned to its statued form.

The vicar let out a heavy, spittle laden sigh and raised the doll to his shoulder. "You're not staying in my church", he said, making his way to the surface.

Marching down across the churchyard, the Reverend Paul said to Miss McAlister and the three men of the village: "You'll not see this abomination walking around again. Its to be locked in the schoolhouse cellar and not removed again. You'll see to it, Headmistress?"

"Of course sir", replied Miss McAlister timidly, "I'll call on the blacksmith this morning to make me a strong lock."

As the doll was thrown down, vociferous wailing could be heard on the upper floors.

"Take me to them!" demanded the vicar. The picture that lay before him in the dormitory was a sorry one. Maria, Sarah and Hannah, in their nightgowns, were sobbing and tearing at their hair.

Seeing the Reverend, Sarah and Hannah drew back. Maria held her ground and said, looking straight in his eyes, "Hell is the cauldron and…", but she was cut short, as the vicar swept the back of his hand across her face.

"Hell is where you belong, if you continue your course!" Turning to Miss McAlister: "These three must leave the school madam - and not return."

"Right away sir", said an awestruck Miss McAlister.

So the girls were bundled away, shipped back to their homes and to other schools. The Reverend, rather revelling in his victory, sermonised one last time the following Sunday on the dangers of entering into pacts with the Devil. And, after a flurry of local interest and bemused onlookers, the village slumbered once more.

And dash their lapstones at its skull
Or prick it with their awl

XIII

[1981]

Louise, Nick and I sat in our kitchen table in the old girl's school, faced with a seemingly invincible foe and our daughter possessed by it.

"So, here's your theory", I said, trying to piece together in my confused mind the torn shreds of gauze that made up the story. "And though it sounds incredible to me, I can rule out nothing now. Not after all we've been through and all we've seen. You're saying Nick that there is a direct connection between the ship The Volta and the Dutch Doll. Somehow, our local squire's son became involved in the slave trade, on the ship on which the doll travelled too. The doll carries a curse laid heavily by the evils that came with the transportation of people into slavery. So much death must have stained it. On one journey, the ship goes down in a storm. Someone makes a misguided connection between the body of a dead son and the doll and...and that's how it ends up in a sleepy village in the middle of England."

"In a nutshell, yes" replied the vicar. "The Dutch Doll was perhaps made from a dark African tree and this, together with its travels across the Atlantic and the trade it was involved in, imbued it with a kind of evil - I think the essence of Satan. This drives it to - and I don't mean to be too melodramatic here - this drives it to claim souls for the Devil."

"Has our Emily been 'claimed'?", Louise asked worriedly.

"I'm sorry, my dear", Nick tried to calm her in his practiced vicarly tone, "I didn't mean to be alarmist. She certainly appears *distracted*, maybe even possessed. But distracted children can be brought back to earth; possessed souls can be freed. Take heart, we should not loose hope."

"But every time we have that wicked woman, Mabel Freeman, and the Dutch Doll within reach, they slip away. They're greased, if you like, unable to be grasped", I said hopelessly.

"Evasive yes, difficult to catch, yes, but not impossible to subdue. You forget that the doll has been encased, fairly successfully, in the church for the last forty or fifty years. It wasn't just iron shackles that prevented it from moving, it was a will, a faith, the same faith that I carry around with me, that contained it. It was that overwhelming force for good that has kept it under control. We can at least try and do that."

"First, though, to find them", I said, bringing my head down into my hands with weary frustration.

"There is a good deal of time for us to look. What's the time now?", Nick queried, looking to the kitchen clock. "Not quite one. Four or five hours 'til dark. And we'll not be the only ones out. The police will be look-

THE DUTCH DOLL

ing too. In some ways though, I'd rather I came across those two than any 'unarmed', ungodly man."

"Will you come up and say some words to Emily first, then we'll clear out again. I don't want her to be in the village anymore; she's much more at risk, much more susceptible, than any of the rest of us."

"Of course I'll come up", Nick said, standing. As we climbed up to Emily's room, he reasoned: "We don't hear any more of those three girls expelled from the school in the eighteen twenties. But I think I did read that they all went away, which may have saved them."

Emily's room was silent and dim; the thick curtains masking the majority of the pale sunlight outside. She lay stiffly, arms by her side outside her covers, eyes open, staring blackly, expressionless, at the ceiling. No glimmer of a reaction to the door opening, or people entering. We were silent too, as though not wishing to break the calm. Although it wasn't calmness that pervaded the room, but menace. Even I, her own father, could find no serenity or sweetness in Emily's composure, just a quiet, seething hatred.

"I'll speak then", said Nick in a half whisper, turning to us parents for approval, which we gave. "Our Lord God, bring peace and light to your daughter, Emily. Bring her from the clutches of the dark, free her from those who would take her away from the true path and show her the way back to you, Lord." As the vicar said this prayer, he lay his hand on Emily's head. His hand shook with what looked like pain, as though he were forcing it to hold a hot coal and when he removed it, which he did swiftly, a redness marked the outline of his fingers and thumb on Emily's forehead. Emily did look to Nick fleetingly, imploringly, as he recoiled, then returning to her blank skyward look.

"My God!" Louise exclaimed, "is she burnt?", feeling Emily's forehead gingerly.

"No, she's not harmed", said Nick, rubbing his palm, "the heat was coming from her."

"And are you alright?", she asked.

"Yes, yes, yes. I'll recover in a moment. But what is obvious is that a strong evil force does possess this girl. Though did you see that there was a flicker of recognition there, as if she wanted to receive help. That is hopeful. All is not lost with this one. But your suggestion - about getting her away again - is one that you should carry out, something you should do now."

As Louise and I gathered together a few things and I carried Emily to the car, she and I spoke about what lay ahead.

"You realise that I have to stay, have to try and see this thing through to the bitter end. Don't you?" I asked.

"Yes", Louise said half-heartedly. "I can see the importance of doing something, of carrying on. I just wish it didn't have to be you. Couldn't Nick get someone else - another parishioner, or even the bishop, to come and bang his iron drum to chase away the ghosts?"

"If there were someone else, I'd join you. But in the time it would take the vicar to convince someone, even a fellow clergyman, that action was needed, someone else could be hurt, someone else...might have...", of course I was about to say 'died' and although Louise knew what word was to come too, we both shied away from it and from the thoughts that it conjured.

"Just don't put yourself in any unacceptable danger, that's all", was all that Louise could say, as I bundled

Emily in the car, wrapped in her blanket. "We need you with us."

"I'll be with you, always", I said, holding Louise's face in my hands and kissing away a tear. "I'll look after myself. I love you...", and we parted, the car speeding off up the Bell Hill.

"I appreciate that must have been hard. And thank you for staying with me again", Nick said, putting his hand on my shoulder. "Right, to arm ourselves again and have a poke around."

We headed back to the church, where Nick refilled his little pill bottles with holy water and checked his torch batteries. "I hope we won't need these, if we can find them before dark", he said.

That afternoon, we made wider and wider sweeps around the church. We set little traps; cotton threads strung at the crypt entrance and at the bookcase in my cellar, to show signs of disturbance. And we returned periodically to find none.

We crossed with police officers who warned us off some paths, but across large tracts of farmland and in the old ironstone quarry, we were unhindered, but unsuccessful. By six o'clock, as the sun was going down, we had no sign, no clue.

"We can be pretty sure that they're not out in the open", Nick surmised, "or we or the police would have stumbled upon them. We should stay in the safest place we can tonight. I've brought a couple of sleeping bags over to the church. There's an old iron furnace by the choir stalls that we can keep on all night."

Back in the Old Hall, there was a new bolt hole, a new refuge for Mabel and the Dutch Doll. The elegant green drawing room, the one in which the first Reverend Paul was received by Sir Thomas Dolben, was abandoned and had slowly decayed into its present state, frayed, faded and empty. But in the corner, amidst a pile of blankets, the two friends looked out into the room, admiring its wonderful decay, congratulating themselves on its obscurity, its out-of-the-way-ness.

Nick and I searched the church from top to bottom, to be absolutely sure that it was occupied by no one but us. We checked behind the organ, in the vestry and climbed the bell tower. Nothing.

"There's no access to the inside of the church from the crypt?" I asked.

"No."

"Then we're alone and all the doors and windows are secure. What should we do if we're somehow enticed outside or hear the noises?"

"We - very cautiously and most importantly, *together* - we investigate", said Nick, explaining exploratory gestures with his hands. "Making first certain that the church is locked up and can't be used to escape into. If they get in here, we'll have the devil of a job containing them."

"They wouldn't come in here, surely?"

"If they can find apparent 'sanctuary' in the crypt, which is consecrated, then...well, it appears that they are not repelled by the building or its significance. What does seem to have an effect is the power of prayer, the word of the scriptures."

"So there's something in the inscription on the scroll that the doll carries - it says 'search the scriptures', doesn't it?", I asked.

"Mmm", the vicar nodded. "There's no doubt something in the bible that holds the key, but it could be one of a hundred thousand passages. The quote 'search the scriptures', comes from St John's Gospel, but I've read and re-read it and can find no solution to today's problem there."

"There's the rhyme, the spell if you like, that came to me in a dream; its one that I've been afraid to say out loud, for fear that it might have a catastrophic effect."

"Then, quite simply, write it out", Nick suggested.

The simplicity of the idea amazed me. "Well yes. Why not? What harm could that do?", so, settling down on the front pew, I jotted down *'Hell is the cauldron and the devil is the spoon'* and handed my scrap of paper to Nick.

Perusing it for a moment, Nick said: "It doesn't come from scripture, but then why would it - it's designed to be against scripture. I'll muse on it for a while, perhaps read the good book for inspiration. It's given plenty before." The vicar took his bible, sat in his sleeping bag, put out a palm to check the heat from the furnace and turned a page or two. I took a silent stroll, skirting the inner walls of the nave, reading epitaphs.

About ten minutes later, as I'd passed the south door, there came a great pounding at it, that made me leap out of my skin.

"Vicar, vicar - help!" It was the voice of Fred, his gardener.

Nick was up in a flash, carefully stowing my slip of paper in his place in the bible and slinging his bag over his shoulder as he walked swiftly down the aisle. "Fred?", he said, as he unbolted the door, "whatever is the matter?" Fred almost threw himself into the church porch, out of breath and looking startled.

"I...I, you see, it occurred to me, when I got home today", he panted, trying to pull himself together, "that

I'd forgotten those seeds I'd promised Mrs Bailey. So I popped back over to the potting shed and...well - you don't think I'll go to hell, do you vicar? You don't think it was *portentous*, do you?"

"Portentous? A bad omen, you mean? What?"

"I saw...I saw the devil's face in the window of the shed. There - I've said it now. Sounds mad, I know and I don't expect you to believe me, but, I've never seen anything as clearly in my life. He was as close as you are to me. The full vision: yellow cats eyes, horns, pointed beard, like a child's picture of Satan, made life. I don't want to die vicar; say it was not a sign, tell me you believe me."

"Now calm down Fred. I do believe you. Plain and simple. The devil is among us. But I don't believe he was after you. He used you to get us to come out. So we will, we're ready for him and his own. You get away now Fred and don't trouble yourself. Go to your house. If you don't hear back from us within two hours, then call the police. They won't be any match for the supernatural evil that we're up against, but they could create a generous distraction. Now go!"

Fred lost no time trotting off through the lych-gate. Nick locked up the church, which was still emblazoned in light, and we headed for the vicar's garden.

"He didn't see the devil, surely?", I asked Nick incredulously as we stepped down into the vicarage garden.

"I've heard more fantastical things - I've seen more hard to imagine things recently. Fred's not easily spooked; he's often around the church after dark. If he says he saw something, he saw it." Nick strode over towards the shed, flicking on a torch with one hand, bible still in the other. I was less keen to come face to face with the antichrist and hung back a bit. Nick tapped the single small pane that formed the window of the shed, then shone his light inside. "Nothing", he shouted back to me. "I don't have a key, but there's one in the vicarage, if you think we should take a closer look."

I shrugged my shoulders, "If it appears empty and it's locked, there's probably no point..." There was a distinct rustling sound coming from the bushes beyond the shed.

"Who's there! Is that you Mabel?" the vicar called, waving his torch in the general direction. The arc caught movement, a black shape retreating to the sound of further rustling of the undergrowth.

"It's them!" I urged, fumbling with my torch and joining Nick to break through the bushes. We found ourselves in thick vegetation, in an overgrown patch of land that once was the ornamental garden of the Old Hall.

"The Hall, of course!", Nick said, amazed at his own stupidity.

"But surely the police have checked here?"

"A cursory peek, maybe, but the building is immense - and you can see the state the gardens are in", Nick said, trying to beat a path to clearer ground.

I scratched my hand pretty badly as it snagged on a briar, "Damnation!" was as far as present company would allow my language to degenerate. "They must've found an easy route through all this."

"No doubt", replied the vicar, "but - here - here's a clearing and...yes, ahead, through there, is the Old Hall. You see?"

"Yes."

We came out facing the southern façade, a wide slab of ornate Tudor carving, just as cloud cleared and moonlight illuminated it. Making our way anti-clockwise around this impressive edifice, we kept our eyes peeled for any movement. There was none. Not a single sign of life. It was as though all life in the grounds had been stifled, or at least banished. Not a single small mammal, not an insect, stirred. Nick motioned me towards the stone porch ahead of us. We cast an eye over the door itself; sturdy, chained, rusted and immovable, complete with a warning sign to intruders.

"If they're in here, they didn't get in this way", Nick observed obviously.

Continuing to skirt around, we came to a boarded window, only...half the boards were scattered on the ground. Nick and I glanced at each other and without a word, he entered by a gingerly placed leg first, then head and shoulders, with the trailing leg swiftly disappearing behind. I put in my torch first for it to be pulled from my hands and switched off. I took a step back. Nick's bible hand beckoned me in. I apprehensively climbed in. He pulled me into the corner of the room and whispered in my ear:

"They're here - I heard footsteps out there", Nick said. As my eyes became accustomed to the fuzzy dark grey, I could make out a door-less frame and a corridor beyond. The room we were in was stripped to the floorboards, with bare wires hanging from the ceiling and plasterwork exploded in a far corner.

We trod carefully across the expanse to the doorway and each looked in opposite directions. No sign; no sound. I pointed to the left, figuring that was the way into the house. Nick nodded his agreement and continued to creep along. There was another sound, like the scraping of a chair on a hard floor, then a girl's laughter. Emily! I immediately thought, but then dismissed this. Yes, she was miles away. The Dutch Doll then. Nick sped up and I was pulled behind. He was completely, single-mindedly, in pursuit. Ahead of us, a glow came from behind a closed door. A flickering light - a fire.

Nick halted us, turned our backs to the door and flicked on his torch. He opened his bible at the page marked by my scrap of paper.

"I think I've found the antidote to that satanic phrase you heard", he said. "I was quite drawn to this, in Judges. It is a way of testing that you belong to one side or another, called shibboleth. We belong to one side...and they another."

"But how do you use it?", I said, puzzled at the obscure bible class at this time.

"I still don't know. But the doll asks us to search the scriptures, I have and this is what I've found. It's the only weapon I have."

"We can't just go in there, with a...Hebrew word!" I whispered my protest. As I did, we both felt a stirring in the air. Dust swirled around us. And the noises, familiar to us both, started up. The chink of light from the closed door flickered more vehemently, with greater intensity. Nick inhaled deeply and strode towards the door. He held onto the doorknob for three full seconds, as the din crashed about us unabated, then wrenched the door open, pushing it so hard that it bashed against the wall as it swung to its full extent. I stood in the doorway with him and beheld a most frightening spectacle.

The Dutch Doll and Mabel were spinning, hands clasped at arms length, in the eye of a small tornado that lifted them clean off the floor. They were singing together their chosen spell, the one that I had written down for the vicar. In their spinning, they saw the door open and the two of us at it, but merely smiled over at us, as would children passing on a merry-go-round. The room around them was alight with colour. There was a roaring, dancing fire in the hearth to the left and, to the right, a large window, down to the ground.

Nick opened his bible at the marked page and began reading: "*Then said they unto him, say Shibboleth; and he said Sibboleth: for he could not frame to pronounce it right. They took him, and slew him at the passages of Jordan: and there fell at that time of the Ephriamites forty and two thousand.*" As he read, the noises subsided and at the word 'Shibboleth', the doll and Mabel gasped and dropped to the ground, like they were jumping from a rolling train.

Nick seized his bottled water and, unstoppering one, threw the contents at Mabel. There was a hiss of steam and we saw that it cut through her skirt like acid. Nick reached for another, but the Dutch Doll beat him to it, knocking his bag out of his hand. It leapt upon him and went to dig at his eyes with its fingers. He was fighting her, shaking his head to avoid being gauged. I scrambled for Nick's bag, drew out another bottle and smashed it onto the doll's back. It rolled off him in agony, writhing. Nick was to his feet again, facing Mabel and the doll, who were retreating towards the fire.

"Say 'shibboleth' for me", Nick urged them and again at the sound of the word, they were aghast and mumbled something incomprehensible to us. "For you and we are of opposing sides, one of good, one of evil. You cannot say shibboleth..." at this second time, the doll stood up, stretching its arms high...and threw itself back into the flames. As it did, I saw that it at once returned to its former, solid, immovable form. And as it did, it appeared to act as a massive incendiary, throwing a powerful explosion, a mixture of yellow flame and black debris outwards. Nick and I were thrown backwards and I was knocked unconscious for a moment.

Waking, I felt cold night air on my face. Nick was standing beside me and we faced the collapsed window and the raging fire within. To our amazement, Mabel stood and walked towards us, oblivious of her own smouldering clothes and hair.

"You thought you'd got the better of me, didn't you?", she snarled, baring teeth as she spoke, "but there's nothing for me to be afraid of, as I know what to do." And once more, as she stepped towards us, she recited: "Hell is the cauldron and the Devil is the spoon", and once more. But at this second time of telling, a great rumbling earthquake mounted and a huge black figure, a full eight feet tall, filling the crumbling window frame, rose up behind Mabel. Just as I had seen in my dream, at the word "Devil", the figure took Mabel by the shoulders, and pulled her down in a terrific thunderbolt, that emptied the space they both occupied, even of air. For a moment, their shape hung in the space. And the final expression on Mabel's face, one of utter surprise and horror, slid away after her.

It was only after that wicked woman had been dragged down, that I began to feel hurt. The explosion must have rocked me quite seriously, I felt. There was a sudden heat burning inside me and I was bathed in sweat. My mind felt without sides and everything I could see seemed distant, as though viewed through the wrong end of a telescope. And something was grabbing at my diaphragm, except that my insides did not feel normal at all. My chest felt as though it was filled with wire wool - fine, abrasive and intrusive. At the centre of my brain, racked and lost in a torturous piece of mathematics, was a tiny hair, representing possession. I slumped back onto my elbows. The vicar supported me.

But that was not all. From the flames the Dutch Doll walked still. On its stumps, blackened by the fire, but with eyes more alive and more wild than I had ever seen. Out towards us.

"Will this thing not die!" yelled Nick, at my side. He let me slip down further and I saw him take his bag from his shoulder one more time. He rose up and in one athletic leap, felled the doll, landing with his foot on its chest. There was a squeal. I saw the vicar leaning over it, quelling its struggles with a knee here, a hand there. He was speaking to it. No, praying over it. And he took out his last remaining bottle of holy water. She was calm by now and he held up her head so she could drink it. Once the bottle was emptied, she smiled a grateful smile and lay back. In a second, she'd burst into flames. Nick jumped back and in his haste, dropped his bible by her. The Dutch Doll reached out for it with shaking hand and quickly pulled it to her burning torso. The small figure finally succumbed, letting her body relax back to the ground, like flesh and blood. And as she did, as the flames from within her grew to a frightening height, we saw the spirits of countless trapped souls, released, like birds freed from a cage. Men, women, boys and girls, mostly girls, flew up from the pyre, accompanied by cascading ashes as the doll peeled, layer after layer. I remember thinking that the fire felt like celebration, as a fire marking the end of war. Before I let go of the ground and the blackness returned.

-- End --